Praise for Serenity Woods's
White-Hot Christmas

"This heartwarming holiday romance is for those who like their sex hot and their endings happy. The relationship between Merle and Neon starts out as a no-strings holiday affair, but when they unexpectedly fall into love, the story packs a surprising emotional wallop. Highly recommended."

~ *Library Journal*

"This [is] a lighthearted, sexy read but a totally enjoyable one. ...I liked the upbeat, modern tone of this book with the fun dialogue topped off with steamy love scenes."

~ *Dear Author*

"I adore the world Ms. Woods has built here, with real and charismatic characters, and a delightful location...one of the best holiday books I have ever read."

~ *Long and Short Reviews*

"The story is well written and watching the two delightful characters break out of their shells keeps every page interesting. Definitely a 'read me' book!"

~ *Fresh Fiction*

Look for these titles by
Serenity Woods

Now Available:

Something Blue
Seven Sexy Sins

Sensual Healing
An Uncommon Sense

Print Anthology
Come Rain or Come Shine

White-Hot Christmas

Serenity Woods

SAMHAIN
PUBLISHING

Samhain Publishing, Ltd.
11821 Mason Montgomery Road, 4B
Cincinnati, OH 45249
www.samhainpublishing.com

Editing by Imogen Howson
Cover by Kendra Egert

First Samhain Publishing, Ltd. electronic publication: November 2011
First Samhain Publishing, Ltd. print publication: October 2012

Dedication

For Tony and Chris, my Kiwi boys.

I'd like to take this opportunity to thank my editor, Immi, who's helped me so much with my writing. I'd also like to thank Ruthie Knox, my critique partner and good friend, who stayed up into the wee small hours reading this book and who taught me how to use commas. ☺ She did a great job considering how hopeless I am, and any grammatical errors are purely down to me.

Chapter One

"Every woman over the age of twenty-five suffers from tinnitus."

Having made this profound statement, Neon Carter heaved a sigh and stretched out on the honey-coloured sand of New Zealand's Ninety-Mile Beach, letting the breeze from the Tasman Sea wash over him and provide some relief from the scorching December sun.

Lying next to him, his cousin Jake raised a hand to shield his eyes from the glare and stared at him, clearly confused. "Eh?"

"Tinnitus. Ringing in the ears. Wedding bells?"

"That sounds like a quote from an old black-and-white fifties comedy."

"That's because it *is* a quote from an old black-and-white fifties comedy. Don't knock the classics."

Jake frowned. "Don't you think you're generalising a bit?"

Neon sighed again, covering his face with an arm, wishing he had his sunglasses. "I guess. It just seems that with every woman I've been out with recently, we get to the third date and they start discussing the colour of the bridesmaids' dresses."

Jake raised an eyebrow. "Was Ella pressing you, then? Bree told me you split up with her."

Neon looked over at him, exasperated. "We dated for three weeks and she wanted her own space in the wardrobe. I mean, she'd not even been to the house."

"Well, of course not. God forbid you actually let a female member of the species onto that hallowed ground."

Neon frowned. "What's that supposed to mean?"

"Nothing." Jake grinned. "I guess they think you're a catch. I have no idea why."

"Thanks."

Jake laughed. He studied his cousin thoughtfully. "I suppose you can't blame them for wanting to snare you. You have your own house, the sort of job women fantasise about and you're not bad looking."

"Thank you for that effusive compliment." Neon shifted uncomfortably in the hot sand and sat up to look longingly at the sea. "Are we going back in? I'm roasting like a Christmas turkey here. Everyone on the beach will be getting out their cranberry sauce."

"Dude, give a guy a break—my arms are like noodles. We've been surfing nonstop for two hours."

"I thought being a newlywed built up your stamina."

Jake grimaced. "Actually, I'm having trouble keeping up with her. She's like a kid with a new Barbie doll for Christmas— she wants to play with me all the time." Then he grinned. "There *are* some advantages to being married."

"Hmm." Neon fell silent and let his gaze drift to the boats on the horizon.

He wasn't opposed to marriage. Quite the opposite, in fact. And Jake's wife certainly hadn't put him off the concept. Bree Cameron—well, Bree Warren now—had a great figure, a sharp brain, a quick wit and an impish smile, and Jake hadn't batted an eyelid before asking her to marry him. Okay, so she wasn't blonde, which was fairly high up on Neon's list of "Top five qualities required in the ideal wife", but he envied his cousin more than he cared to admit. He'd be happy to settle down with the right woman and get married, have kids, the whole package deal, some day. But not yet, and certainly not with a woman he'd only been dating for three weeks. It took months, maybe even years, to make sure you were compatible for life—didn't it?

He looked over at Jake. "How long had you known Bree before you realised you wanted to marry her?"

Jake laid an arm across his eyes. "About thirty minutes. Give or take." Neon swore at him, and Jake shrugged. "I'm serious. You'll understand one day. You'll turn around and see her—the one woman you're meant to be with—and she'll knock you for six straight off the bat."

"No cricket analogies, Jake, you know I hate the game."

"Don't change the subject."

Neon sighed. "Come on, what you've got is unusual. It doesn't happen to everyone."

"More than you think. It's called falling in love, and it exists—why else are there so many songs written about it? You may have escaped Cupid's clutches so far, but he's got his arrow set on you, my friend. And don't come crying to me when you beg her to marry you and she accuses you of having tinnitus."

Neon laughed. "Fair enough. I'll be happy to step in front of his bow when the time comes along. But until Ms. Right turns up, what do I do? I could understand it if I'd been going out with a girl for a couple of years and she was getting twitchy, but three weeks? I feel so bad when I back off and they get all upset."

Jake shrugged. "You could try not dating any more women

until you find her."

Neon frowned. "How will I find her if I'm not dating anyone?"

"I told you, you'll know as soon as you set eyes on her. Just abstain from sex until then."

"You're kidding me? I might not meet her till I'm fifty."

"So?"

"Jake, I'm not staying celibate for the next twenty-three years." Neon sighed. "I happen to like sex. What I need to do is find a girl who likes it as much as I do but who's not booking the church as soon as I take her out to dinner."

Jake laughed. "Sounds like you're in need of a holiday romance."

"Oh yeah." Neon tipped his face up to the sun. "Hot sex and no worries about getting serious. Sounds ideal." He glanced across at his cousin. "Hey, wait a minute. Isn't your sister-in-law arriving this afternoon? Strange name like Pearl or Twirl or something?"

Jake looked at him warily. "Her name's Merle, and you can forget about making a move on her. Bree would kill me if she thought I was setting her up with you."

"What's Bree got against me? I thought she liked me?"

"She does like you—she just wouldn't want Mr. Anti-Commitment anywhere near her sister."

Neon frowned. "I'm not anti-commitment. I'm anti-three-week-commitment."

Jake sighed. "It doesn't matter. Merle's a regular bluestocking, not your type at all."

"Hold on, where are you from, 1952? Who the hell uses the term 'bluestocking' anymore?"

"It fits Merle perfectly," said Jake wryly. "She's a university lecturer in archaeology, of all things, elegant, cool and as British as cucumber sandwiches. And there's absolutely no way she'd ever consider a holiday romance, so you can wipe that look off your face."

"I haven't got a look on my face."

"Yes, you have, you've got that *hmm, sounds like a challenge* look."

Neon grinned. "Well, hmm, it sounds like a challenge."

Jake sat up, the sand sticking to his wet skin, making it look like a sheet of sandpaper. "Seriously, she's only in New Zealand for two weeks. She works really hard, and she looks after Bree's mum—she just needs to relax while she's here."

"Hey, I'm only thinking of the young lady. What better way is there to relax than to have wild holiday sex?" Neon laughed at the look on Jake's face. "It's all right, I won't make a move on her, I promise. But can I ask you one thing—if my natural charm works its magic and *she* propositions *me*, can I say yes?"

Jake smiled. "Believe me, I know Merle. There's absolutely no way she'd ever sleep with anyone without dating them for six months first. She's not exactly what you'd call impulsive."

"She's not met me yet." Neon winked at him. "I have animal magnetism."

"If that animal's a skunk, yeah."

Neon pretended to look offended. "A hundred bucks says she's in love with me before the end of her holiday."

"Done." They shook hands on it. Then they both burst out laughing.

Neon picked up a shell and threw it into the sea. In spite of his teasing, there was no way he'd make a move on Bree's sister—he was far too fond of both Bree and his cousin for that. And anyway, just because she was Bree's sibling didn't mean she'd be as gorgeous as Jake's wife. He didn't normally go for the intellectual type. She probably wouldn't appeal to him at all.

He sighed. Enough of this sitting around. He put Merle Cameron to the back of his mind and got to his feet. Doing nothing didn't come naturally to Neon. The sea was too blue, the white foam too attractive for him to continue to laze about. He picked up his board. "Are you going to lie around like a stranded whale all day or are you hitting the surf with me?" He kicked sand over his cousin, who yelled at him and picked up his own board, running down the beach after him and plunging into the sea.

They swam out past the breakers, ready for the rollers heading toward them, and spent a pleasant half an hour surfing, tiring themselves out on the powerful waves.

"Last one," Jake yelled out finally. "Bree's car's just pulled up."

Neon nodded, ready for a drink and a five-minute laze on the sand. Together they popped up on the boards, catching the surf and riding the white foam toward the beach. He steadied himself on the board, feeling the exhilaration that never grew old as the wave lifted him and bore him toward the sand.

He glanced up at the skyline and did a double take. A woman stood on the shore, watching him, her hand raised to shield her eyes from the blinding glare.

The rest of the girls on the beach wore bikinis or T-shirts and shorts, some with a baseball cap, bodies bronzed from a lifelong gradual exposure to the sun. This girl's skin was pale, and she wore a flowy dress that fluttered in the light breeze, clinging to her curvy figure. Presumably she had no idea the dress was transparent with the sun behind her, and he could see the outline of her long, long legs. With her wide-brimmed hat, her blonde hair lifting beneath it like a scarf, she looked as if she'd stepped off the set of a nineteenth-century English drama.

He registered all this in a split second—but it was long enough to break his concentration. The board slid under him as he shifted his weight, and with a curse, he fell backward into the foam.

Merle Cameron watched with amusement as the taller of the two surfers tumbled into the sea. She'd been drinking in the beauty of her holiday destination, her toes sinking into the soft sand, the tension in her shoulders—which had been building over the several days she'd spent travelling—slowly beginning to ooze away. The air tasted salty and clean, and her spirits lifted at the sight of the seagulls and the smell of a barbecue from farther along the beach. She couldn't believe it was the twenty-second of December. A hot Christmas—how odd was that? Talk about an upside-down country.

"Where's Jake?" she'd asked her sister, scanning the beach, and Bree had pointed out to sea.

Merle had followed her gaze, looking out over the glistening water at the two surfers, thinking how effortless they made it look as they popped up easily on the boards. Now, however, she smiled at the clumsy display. Even she could fall off more elegantly than that.

"Wow." Bree put her hand up to shield her eyes from the sun. "Something must have distracted Neon. He's usually stuck to that board with superglue."

"Neon?" Merle watched Jake skid to a stop on the sand, jump off the board and pick it up, then walk up the beach toward them.

"Jake's cousin," Bree explained. "It's short for Napoleon, but don't tell him I told you or he'll kill me." She walked forward and put her arms around her husband, giving him a hug in spite of his wet body.

Merle waited, smiling, thinking how great they looked together. Jake had been so good for Bree. Handsome in a boy-next-door kind of way, with slightly curly brown hair, he was down-to-earth and sensible, a suitable balance for Bree, whose impulsiveness had got her into trouble in the past.

Jake detached himself from his wife and came over and kissed Merle on the cheek.

"It's so good to see you," he said, grinning.

She laughed. "You look well. Marriage agrees with you." She wasn't kidding either—Jake glowed with health and well-being, his skin deeply tanned and glistening where it wasn't covered with sand.

"It certainly does." He grabbed Bree and planted a kiss on her shoulder. "Thank you for giving your sister to me."

"It was good to get rid of her. She only ever drove me mad anyway."

He laughed, turning as Neon finally approached the three of them. "Stylish landing," Jake said, amused.

"Not quite the entrance I'd hoped to make." Neon shook his head, sending droplets scattering. "But then someone distracted me." He looked over at Merle, his smile making it clear she'd been the one to claim his attention. "You must be Bree's sister. I'm Neon." He held out a wet hand.

"I'm Merle." She offered her own hand, conscious of his compliment. He gripped hers in a firm handshake, his brown skin making hers look absurdly white. A tingle ran all the way down her spine at the physical contact. As he released her hand, Merle couldn't help but let her gaze roam over him. He was *gorgeous*. And huge! Three or four inches taller than Jake—and she knew her brother-in-law was six foot—Neon had broad shoulders and a muscular, deeply tanned body, with a striking black Māori tattoo circling his upper left arm. The tips of his light brown hair were golden from the sun, and as her gaze settled on his face she saw he had the most beautiful deep brown eyes that crinkled very slightly at the edges with half a dozen laughter lines.

He looked her over at the same time, his gaze skimming down her figure and back up to her face. When his eyes met hers, they were filled with lazy admiration.

Jake cleared his throat. Merle suddenly realised she'd been staring as if she'd met a movie star, and heat rose in her cheeks.

Neon studied her, then looked up at the sky, shading his eyes. "Warm day, isn't it?"

"Very," she agreed, realising he was trying to cover up her blush. How nice. He didn't fool her sister, though. Bree began to walk up the beach, not even bothering to hide her amused smile.

Merle bit her lip and turned to follow her but didn't miss the way Jake elbowed his cousin in the ribs and the playful push Neon gave him back. She lowered her eyes, trying not to laugh. What were they, twelve? It was fun for a moment, to pretend to be ten or fifteen years younger, thinking about nothing but boys. Real life was so much more demanding. She gave a sigh, turning her attention to the scene before her. It had been a pretty intense year, and she'd managed to escape her demanding life by the skin of her teeth, and then only for two weeks. She desperately needed to relax.

When was the last time she'd had a holiday? Worryingly, she couldn't remember. She'd had that weekend away with Phil over a year ago, but it had only been to Cornwall, and he'd spent most of it on the phone, sorting out some case with his partner at the law firm. The last time she'd actually got away, out of the country, to somewhere warm and foreign, had been while her father was alive, more than three years ago. That had been to Minorca, and Bree had come with them. It had only been a package deal, basic bed and board, hardly the holiday of a lifetime, but the landscape and climate had been hot and alien, and they'd all enjoyed the seafood, the warm sea and the golden sand. It had been the last time they'd been happy as a family.

"No unhappy thoughts are allowed in New Zealand," Neon stated, surprising her. She hadn't realised he'd drawn alongside her and was watching her as she gazed out to sea.

She glanced at him, seeing his eyes were kind, thoughtful. "Sorry. I was thinking about my father. He'd have loved it here." She smiled at how exotic the scene looked from a British perspective, the sea a startling blue, Neon and Jake fit and tanned, surfboards under their arms. It was quiet and peaceful, the only sound the cry of the seagulls and the squeal of children as they ran in and out of the waves—not that there were many people on the beach. In what she was beginning to recognise as true Kiwi style, only half a dozen families dotted the golden sand, enjoying the sunshine. "You'd never get this kind of view at Margate."

He laughed. "I'm guessing England's beaches aren't its best selling point."

"Let's just say similar weather in the UK would bring people out the way jam draws ants. You wouldn't be able to move on the seafront. Have you ever been to the UK?"

"No."

"Well, don't bother. You wouldn't like it." As the words left her mouth, she realised how arrogant she sounded and flashed him an apologetic smile—who was she to say what he would or wouldn't like? But he didn't seem to mind.

"You're probably right." He bent to pick up a stone, brushed the sand off it, looking at the colours, then skimmed it into the ocean. "Jake wasn't impressed."

"What did he say about it?"

"I think his exact words were 'It's fucking cold'." She burst out laughing and he joined in. Then he brushed the sand off his hands and sent her a wry look. "Sorry. I've only just met you and I'm insulting your country. I'm sure it's got many redeeming qualities. I'd love to visit some of the historical sites—we haven't got anything like that here, apart from Waitangi and the Stone Store, and they're hardly ancient."

"Its history is its main attraction, I think," she said. "Unfortunately, though, many of the places are overrun by tourists, and it's difficult to get a sense of atmosphere." She went to say more, but they were approaching a group of about seven or eight other men and women sprawled out on towels, soaking up the sun, and Jake had walked up next to her.

"Come and meet the rest of the gang."

Merle smiled nervously as Jake led her up to the rest of the party. Bree had told her they were staying in a beach house that night with some friends, and Merle had nearly decided to stay behind in Kerikeri. She wasn't keen on parties or socialising in general and felt out of her depth in this country with the athletic, tanned women who were comfortable prancing around in the tiniest bikinis. But as she approached, everyone sat up, smiling, and when Jake introduced her, the chorus of hellos made her feel welcome.

Bree shook out the two towels she'd brought from the car and collapsed on one, indicating for Merle to sit beside her. She did so, stretching out her legs and leaning back, letting the sun warm her through. It had been a cold autumn in England, with snow in November, and she'd thought she'd never be warm again.

"Beer? Or Diet Coke?"

Neon crouched beside a cooler, holding up two bottles.

"A beer would be lovely." She didn't normally drink it, but the idea of a cold lager appealed in the heat.

He twisted off the top and handed it to her, and she thanked him. Nodding, giving her a smile, he stood and walked off with Jake to where some of the guys were starting to throw a Frisbee around.

Merle glanced across at her sister. Bree had been watching them, and now raised her eyebrows and laughed.

"What?" said Merle. "He was just being nice."

"Yes, he was. He also wants to rip all your clothes off."

Chapter Two

Merle felt her cheeks flush red for the second time in about ten minutes. "Oh, for goodness' sake. We were just talking."

Bree's eyes danced with amusement. "I think you've been out of the dating game too long, sis. If you're missing signals like that, no wonder you're still single."

"I'm single by choice."

"Hmm." Bree gave her a look. "Have you had sex at all since you split up with Phil?"

"That's none of your business," Merle said, big-sister fashion, fixing her with a firm look.

"Oh my God." Bree rolled her eyes. "Merle, seriously, are you aware that real penises don't vibrate?"

"Bree!"

Her sister laughed out loud, reached across and patted Merle's knee. "I'm sorry, I can't help it, you're so easy to tease!"

Merle said nothing, looking out to sea. Bree's statement had touched a sore spot. It had indeed been over a year since she'd had sex, and though she would never have admitted it to Bree, she missed the intimacy, even though Phil had hardly set her alight in bed.

Bree reached out and grasped her hand. "I'm sorry, that wasn't fair. I know it's been a difficult year for you."

"Just a bit." Merle glanced across at her sister. "You should call Mum more often."

Bree dropped her hand, turning her face up to the sun. "She depresses me. The more I ring, the more depressed I get."

"I know, but she misses you so. She's just lonely, Bree, and she's not well, you mustn't forget that."

"I know she's not well, but that's no excuse for being so horrible to me." When she looked over, Bree's eyes were cold. "And to Jake. You don't know everything she said to us before we moved out here. She was nasty, Merle. I haven't forgiven her for that."

"I know. It was only because she didn't want to lose you."

"I don't care. You don't say those kinds of things to your daughter when she's getting married. She should have seen how excited I was and been happy for me. And anyway, she could come and visit. It's not all down to me."

Merle said nothing, absently watching Neon as he stretched up for the Frisbee, catching it easily, sending it spinning to one of the others with a flick of his wrist. Bree didn't really have any idea what effect the illness had had on their mother. The cancer, jealousy and fear had eaten Susan from the inside out, and she was a shadow of the woman she'd once been. She would never be able to manage the twenty-six-hour plane journey, physically or mentally. And even if she were able to make the flight, she was just as stubborn as Bree and would never consent to visiting New Zealand. She would see it as giving in, accepting that Bree had been right to choose her husband over her mother.

Susan hadn't always been this way. But the shock of the illness, combined with losing her husband a few years before, had seemed to lower her threshold of resistance and change her personality. She'd had the mastectomy and the cancer had apparently vanished, but she insisted she could feel it inside her, and Merle could almost see the dark hand of the disease still hovering over her mother, twisting her conception of the world and warping her love for her daughters.

"You do too much for her," said Bree.

"She needs looking after."

"She's learned to rely on you. She's not an invalid, Merle. But she is manipulative and devious. She's got her claws in you and she's not going to let you go easily, you do know that, don't you?"

Merle spoke sharply. "Don't talk about her like that, you know it upsets me. And anyway, I'm happy to look after her. I don't need a lecture on how to run my life."

Bree sighed. "I'm not giving you a lecture. I hate to see you not being able to live your life because of her. I mean, I know she had something to do with you splitting up with Phil, didn't she?"

Merle said nothing. Bree was right that their mother had been the reason she and Phil split up, but it hadn't been her mother's fault. If anything, Susan had been a catalyst, an excuse for both her and Phil to bring to an end a relationship that had gradually petered out, like a firework that blazed briefly before dwindling to a gentle spark and finally a dull glow. Except it hadn't really blazed that much in the first place. She'd agreed to go out with Phil because she'd been lonely, and even though their affection had eventually turned physical, she couldn't honestly say in the bedroom they'd done anything but fizzle damply.

She hadn't been as upset when they broke up as she'd thought she'd be when ending her first long-term relationship. Although she'd cried afterward, if she was honest, she knew it wasn't because she missed him but because she was afraid she'd never meet a man who would make her feel the depth of emotion she longed for.

Bree took her silence as affirmation. "I knew it. I'm amazed she let you go long enough to come over here for a fortnight."

Merle stared out to sea. Susan had begged her not to go, but Merle so wanted to see her sister that in the end she'd lost her temper with her mother, which she now regretted, guilt hovering like storm clouds. But it had been an exhausting term at work, and the weather had been bitterly cold. She'd been desperate to escape to somewhere warm, where she could have some freedom, even if it was temporary.

She sighed. "The last year hasn't been much fun. Phil wasn't exactly Casanova, but I did at least get out of the house with him."

"I'm glad you're here." Bree reached over and squeezed her hand.

Merle smiled. Unbidden, her gaze sneaked to Neon, and she watched him standing with hands on hips, talking to Jake, his back to her. She took the opportunity to admire him, noting his long legs, strong shoulders and muscled arms. He must work out. And she absolutely *adored* tall men. At five-foot-ten, she didn't often meet guys who towered over her.

He glanced over his shoulder suddenly, looking right at her, and, flustered, she looked away.

"You like him, don't you?" said Bree.

"I think your husband's lovely." Merle brushed sand from her skirt, deliberately misunderstanding.

"I meant—"

"I know what you meant." Merle sighed. "I'm terrible with men, Bree. I do try. I go out for dinner, or to the theatre, or the cinema. But I always end up thinking they're idiots, and after two or three dates I call it off."

"But you do like Neon."

Merle looked across at her, and was unable to stop her lips curling. "Yes, of course I do. He's gorgeous. But, sweetie, I live on the opposite side of the world. The last thing I need is to get myself caught up in the complication of a long-distance relationship."

Bree shrugged. "Who said anything about a relationship? If I wanted to find you a husband, Neon would be the last person I'd pick. His middle name's 'Feral'. But if you want to get laid... He's pretty good, by all accounts." She winked at Merle. "You know it rusts up if you don't use it." She laughed at the indignant look on Merle's face. "Your problem is you're aiming too high. You need to get back in the saddle. Stop thinking about long-term relationships and concentrate on sex." Her gaze slid across to the guys. She looked back at Merle and waggled her eyebrows.

"A one-night stand?" Merle looked at her, horrified. "Oh my God, I couldn't."

Bree shrugged. "You're halfway across the world where nobody knows you—apart from me and Jake. It's the perfect opportunity to drop your professorial act and turn into a complete tramp. Who's gonna know, for God's sake?"

"How about me? And you and Jake? For a start."

Bree snorted. "Well, I don't care, and we just don't tell Jake." She glanced across at her sister, a gleam in her eye. "I bet you aren't brave enough to have sex on holiday, with a complete stranger."

"I beg your pardon?"

"Stop being so bloody English, Merle. Loosen up a bit."

"Ever heard of AIDS? And STDs? And pregnancy?" Merle's

back was ramrod straight with indignation.

"So use a frickin' condom! Sis, you seriously need to loosen up. You're so tight-laced you're practically wearing a girdle."

Merle sighed, looking at her sister. She knew what Bree was trying to say. The younger girl's hair hung loose and tangled around her tanned shoulders. She wore an old, faded orange T-shirt and denim cutoffs, and she looked blissfully happy with her new life. Merle looked away, fighting an uncharacteristic surge of envy.

Bree studied her sister. "If you get yourself laid over the next fortnight, I'll give you fifty bucks."

Merle stared at her. "Twenty-five pounds? For my good reputation? Are you kidding me?"

"Fifty bucks for every time you get laid. And Merle—if you manage it five times, I'll make it a round three hundred."

Merle's eyes widened. "Are you serious? You're going to pay me to have sex?"

"No, I'm going to pay you to have fun. God knows you need it." She motioned with her head toward Neon. "Imagine it, Merle. Wild holiday sex with a rugby-playing, surfing firefighter."

"He's a firefighter?" She stared at him. That would explain the physique.

"Every girl's dream." Bree grinned. "So are you going to accept?"

Merle said nothing for a moment. He wasn't her sort at all. She went out with intellectuals. Men—usually quite a bit older than her—called Richard or William or Edward, who wore glasses and suits and sardonic smiles. Doctors and lawyers, whose physical activity extended to the occasional game of squash. Not young firefighters with ridiculous nicknames, who wore nothing but rather faded shorts. She doubted he could even spell "intellectual". She went after men's minds, not their tanned bodies, muscular arms and lazy, sexy smiles...

Oh come on, let's be honest. Neon was hot enough to melt gold. Was the size of his brain relevant at all?

Impishly, she imagined kissing him, feeling his hand brushing up her thigh. Was she brave enough to take her sister up on her bet? Sex with a complete stranger? Merle closed her eyes momentarily, unable to believe she was even contemplating the crazy notion. It was the absolute, total opposite of anything she'd ever consider, the twelve midday to her twelve midnight, the South Pole to her North. Merle was a lecturer in archaeology, she was respected, dignified. She was bloody English, for God's sake. She didn't proposition complete strangers.

But the idea was like plastic wrap imbued with static—she couldn't shake it off.

It was such a compelling thought, that was the problem. No strings, no worries about being right for each other, or whether you had anything in common, or deep discussions on the meaning of relationships. Just hot, breathless, sweaty sex with a hunky firefighter. The type of sex she'd seen in Hollywood movies. Fantasy sex, as opposed to rather dull, awkward, rarely inspirational, real-life sex. Somehow she just *knew* Neon would be good in bed. Something to do with his sexy smile. The thought made her feel faint.

She shook her head. This wasn't her at all. She dated for weeks before she ventured near the bedroom. She didn't have sex on the first date, and certainly not with someone she hardly knew. It was ridiculous. It was totally out of the question.

"Don't be stupid," she snorted in answer to Bree's raised eyebrow as the guys began to walk toward them. "And for God's sake, don't say anything."

Bree sighed. "Of course I won't. Relax, Merle. If you want to shut up shop down there, I'm not going to stop you."

"Bree—" But she had to end the conversation because the guys were too close. She satisfied herself with glaring at her sister, even though it was lost on her as she lay back and closed her eyes.

Neon threw himself on the sand next to Merle, picked up a pair of dark sunglasses and slipped them on. He stretched out, humming to a song playing on the radio. In spite of her promise to forget Bree's bet, her gaze lingered on his muscular arms and solid legs, tanned and scattered with light brown hair. He was the complete opposite of the two men she'd gone to bed with in the past. Simon had been tall and skinny, and white as a snowflake in the English tradition, and while Phil had been broader, he could hardly have been called a candidate for surfer of the year. And neither of them had been particularly skilled in the sex area. Oh for a man who knew what he was doing in the bedroom...

Suddenly she realised she couldn't see Neon's eyes and wondered whether he was looking at her, watching her size him up. She stuck her tongue out at him and he rewarded her with a chuckle. He had indeed been watching her. *Crap.* She took a swig from her bottle, blushing again.

He cleared his throat. "How long have you been over here?"

She looked at him, wiping her mouth on the back of her hand. "Only a few days. I haven't been to New Zealand before, so I thought I'd see a bit of Auckland before I flew up."

"What did you think of it?"

"It's a nice city, lots of trees. I liked the museum on the domain."

"Sounds like you lived it up," Bree teased.

"Oh, I did other stuff—went to bars and picked up a couple of desperate men, visited a brothel, you know, the usual."

Neon and Jake laughed.

"You can be less English without sinking to those depths," Bree said, amused.

"Well, I didn't walk around wearing a bowler hat and carrying an umbrella or anything." Merle shot her sister an exasperated glance, irritated, her sister's comment about shutting up shop still rankling. "Anyway, there's nothing wrong with being English."

"Unless you count Morris Dancing," said Neon. "I've always wanted to see a performance. Will you give us a demonstration?"

Still annoyed, she couldn't stop the sarcastic retort as she turned the glare on him. "Not tonight, Josephine." Would he realise she was making reference to the fact that she knew his full name?

Neon stared at her, raised his sunglasses and glared at Bree.

"It's not her fault," said Merle, not wanting to get her sister in trouble. "I made an intelligent guess. I mean, Neon? It's not really a name, is it?"

He looked at her, fixing her with his brown-eyed stare. "You can talk. Proud Titania."

Bree burst out laughing at the look on Merle's face. Jake looked from one to the other, confused. "What?"

Bree grinned. "Mum's a Brontë nut and my sister's named after Merle Oberon, the actress in the old 1930s version of *Wuthering Heights*. And Oberon's in *A Midsummer Night's Dream*."

"Oh." The joke had gone over Jake's head.

"You look shocked I've heard of her." Neon studied Merle's face, obviously amused.

"I'm more surprised you've heard of Shakespeare."

"Ooh." Jake winced.

Bree laughed out loud. "That was a bit below the belt."

Neon's lips curled. "Course I have. Wilfred and I are like that." He crossed his fingers.

Wilfred? Merle opened her mouth to correct him, saw his smile and realised he was teasing her. She met his gaze, seeing the amusement in his eyes, and almost hidden, the hurt. She'd insulted his intelligence, unfairly it seemed. She looked away, embarrassed. What was wrong with her? She wasn't normally rude or irritable like this. It must be the jet lag. That and the fact that Bree always knew how to get under her skin, prodding at her sensitive areas as a kid might poke at a snail with a stick.

"We're going up to the cafe for some lunch," said one of the other men in the group. "You guys coming?"

"Yeah, sure." Jake stood and pulled his wife up. Merle went to get up but saw Neon standing above her, hand extended. She sighed and took it. He lifted her easily, and she stumbled against him.

"Sorry." She brushed sand from her dress, wishing he would realise she was apologising for the insult as well.

"No worries." He met her gaze briefly. He smiled, but his eyes were cool. He turned away, collecting up the empty beer bottles, giving her a perfect view of his tight ass.

She swallowed and looked away, shaking the sand from her towel and rolling it up for Bree. How she longed to be the sort of person who had one-night stands. Why couldn't she be impulsive, carefree and abandoned? She wished she could throw off her reserved image and live in the moment. Bree did—she was remarkably relaxed and happy-go-lucky, so it wasn't as if it was impossible. But she could never be like her sister.

Could she?

Merle bit her lip, excitement sweeping through her. She wasn't really considering this, was she? She wasn't thinking of suggesting hot, meaningless sex with a complete stranger?

As a group, they walked up to the local cafe. On the way, she chatted to David and Ryan, a couple of the other men in the group. They were both friendly and flirted lightly with her, making her laugh. Mischievously, she considered each of them with Bree's idea of holiday sex in mind, but although they were young, strong and beautifully tanned, neither of them came close to Neon on the scale of gorgeousness. He talked to Jake as they walked. He'd pulled on a deep red T-shirt, but was barefoot like most of them in the group. He was the perfect image of a healthy New Zealand man, the sort you saw on holiday adverts. He must have a girlfriend. But surely Bree wouldn't have suggested him if he did?

As they approached the cafe, Jake asked her what she wanted to eat. She felt a wave of tiredness from the jet lag, and just requested a lemonade and an ice lolly, desperate for something cool. She took the opportunity to visit the ladies', splashing water on her face, hoping to perk herself up.

On her way back to the entrance, she heard Jake and Neon at the counter, talking. She paused in the passageway at the mention of her name.

"So, what do you think of Merle?" Jake said.

"She's gorgeous." Neon's compliment took her by surprise. "But I don't think she likes me much. Fair enough. I guess you were right—I'm not the sort of guy a university lecturer would find attractive."

She closed her eyes, cringing as she thought of how she'd put him down. His next words, however, made her eyes fly open.

"I can see what you meant about her, by the way. She's so British and puritanical it's like she's stepped straight out of the English Civil War."

"What did I tell you?" Jake laughed.

Merle's cheeks flamed. Puritanical? How dare he make such a judgement about her when he didn't even know her?

Then she thought about what she'd said to him, about being surprised he'd heard of Shakespeare. She'd insulted him. He was right—she *was* reserved, aloof and snobbish. She completely deserved his comment.

But deep down, she wasn't a prude, and she wasn't cold. She walked back through the cafe, chewing her lip. She longed to throw off the frosty British image she obviously portrayed. How could she show Neon a passionate, sexy woman lay beneath her cool exterior?

Exiting the cafe, she saw he'd chosen a chair to one side of the group, looking out across the sea, and she took a seat opposite him. At that moment his mobile started ringing. Pulling the phone from his shorts pocket, he flipped it open. He looked at the number and hesitated. Sighing, he pressed the answer button, held the phone to his ear, stood up and walked a short distance away.

Merle sipped her lemonade. He glanced over at Jake, who mouthed, "Ella?" Neon nodded and rolled his eyes.

Bree leaned closer to Jake and whispered, "I saw her a couple of days ago. She's gutted he broke up with her. I think she thought she'd got her claws into him. I didn't like to say she shouldn't have discussed the colour card she wanted for the invitations before they'd even been together three weeks."

Merle studied him, playing with her straw. So he was wary about being tied down. Well, who wasn't? She too had backed off when Simon had started murmuring about engagement rings to her, and that was after six months of dating, not three weeks.

Neon tucked his left hand into his pocket, and his elbows were tight against his chest. His whole stance showed his irritation.

When he spoke, however, his voice was gentle and polite. "I know. I'm sorry." He went quiet again, listening to the woman on the other end. At one point he held the phone away from his ear, wincing. Merle could hear Ella screeching at him. She stared, shocked. What on earth had possessed her to react in such a way? No wonder the guy was anti-commitment if his ex-girlfriends treated him like this.

Still, he didn't raise his voice. Merle heard him speak gently but firmly for a while, sighing occasionally before saying goodbye, flipping the phone shut. He paused for a moment before turning around. Then he sat, lowered his sunglasses and looked out to sea. Merle narrowed her eyes. He needed cheering up. What could she do to help?

Neon mused on his conversation with Ella, sliding down in his seat, his arms crossed. He'd never promised her anything, but she'd still demanded more than he could—or wanted to— give. What was it with women? It was enough to make a man want to turn gay. He glanced across at Merle and watched as she crossed her long legs, raising her dress a little to let the sun get to them. Okay, maybe not. But at that moment, he didn't think he ever wanted to date again. Sex, yes. Dating, no. Shame one rarely came without the other, unless you counted paying for it, and he wasn't a big fan of that.

He watched the English girl from behind his dark glasses, turning his head so it looked as if he were staring out to sea. He wasn't quite sure how he felt about her. Her sharp retort on his literary knowledge had stung. She'd thought him ignorant and illiterate because of the way he looked and the job he did, although she had apologised afterward, even if it was in a roundabout way. Obviously her prejudice was her problem, but still... She'd made a judgement about him with no solid foundation.

He sipped his beer, phasing in and out of the conversation, wondering if Ella was still crying or if it had just been put on to make him feel guilty. He didn't miss her. He knew it was cruel, but she'd been a stopgap for him, a warm body when he'd been lonely. He'd never really felt anything deep for her. Hell, he'd hardly had time for his feelings to develop. He wasn't proud of hurting her, especially when he knew she'd been crazy about him, but he couldn't change the way he felt.

He focussed on Merle again. It was a shame she was so haughty, because if he thought about her in a purely physical way, she was very enticing. Long, long legs, curvy body. Beautiful bouncy blonde hair with a hint of red—strawberry blonde, didn't they call it? Smooth skin, with a scattering of freckles. He usually favoured athletic women with a healthy tan and tight, toned bodies, and Merle didn't fit that category—she probably hadn't seen a surfboard in real life before, let alone stood on one. But her womanly figure and pale skin were enticing, and with her floppy hat and sundress she looked elegant, refined. Not too refined, though. He could imagine running his suntanned hand up her smooth white thigh and then farther up her body, cupping her heavy white breast. Hmm. Better not go too far down that road or everyone would become aware of his rising interest.

At that moment, however, his attention was drawn to the

way she'd started eating her ice lolly. She'd unwrapped the frozen ice on a stick and was busy catching the drops with her tongue where it had started to melt. She ran her tongue very slowly up the long length of the lolly—which was amusingly phallic shaped, or was it his imagination?—from the base to the top, which she then covered with her mouth. He stared. She listened to Bree talk, unaware of the suggestiveness of her actions, and did it again, turning the lolly around and licking the base with her pink tongue, then brushing the cold pole all the way up. Against his will, blood rushed to his groin.

He lifted his sunglasses onto the top of his head for a better look, wondering if he'd imagined it. Did she know how erotic she looked? Nobody else seemed conscious of it. He watched, intrigued, holding his breath, as she sucked with her beautiful soft lips at the base, then ran her tongue up it a third time, right to the top. She covered the tip with her mouth, sucking gently. He nearly groaned out loud. She did it again and again, and each time he felt himself harden a little more until he knew if she looked at his thin shorts, she would be in no doubt of his arousal.

She circled her tongue around the tip several times before plunging the lolly between her lips again. By this time, he was incapable of speech and could only stare as, to his shock, she slid the ice lolly into her mouth, taking the whole length of it in, almost to the stick. It was such a wanton, erotic display, he nearly swore out loud.

At that moment, she looked over at him. He stared, waiting for her to grow embarrassed and look away or, even worse, glare at him. She didn't, though, and he suddenly realised she knew he had been watching her and knew exactly what she was doing.

She pulled the lolly slowly out of her mouth, leaving her lips glistening. She licked them, watching him with a bold, enticing stare. Then, quite clearly, she swallowed.

Neon closed his eyes. He tipped his head back until it met the wall with a thud, struggling to control the lust spiralling through him. Jeez, she'd nearly made him come in his shorts, little minx. It took a few moments of deep breathing to calm himself. When he felt in control again, he opened his eyes and looked up at the sky with a sigh, then glanced over to see Jake watching him, puzzled. A wry smile on his lips, he finally looked back at Merle. She laughed and winked at him.

"Wicked girl," he mouthed, unable to stop himself smiling.

She shrugged and continued to lick the lolly, albeit in a less suggestive manner, but her eyes remained on him, lit with mischief. There was more to this prim British chick than met the eye.

Merle had enjoyed teasing him. And the sight of him closing his eyes and tipping his head back was the sexiest thing she'd ever seen. She could imagine that was how he'd look when he came, the thought making her dizzy as she pictured him on top of her, arching into her.

Oh for the love of... Bree was to blame for this. Her sister had turned her into a nymphomaniac.

Not that she could imagine any woman thinking about anything else when they looked at Neon. He was sex on a stick, built for lovemaking, pure and simple.

The waitress had brought out the food and everyone tucked in, hungry after a morning spent surfing and playing. Merle nibbled on a chunky fry, smiling as she saw Neon take bite after bite out of a huge sandwich. Gosh, the man could eat! But then look at his size—a Rav 4x4 needed more fuel than a Mini, didn't it?

She looked across at Bree, who held up a hand, fingers

spreading, mouthing the word "Fifty". Merle shot her a glare but couldn't stop herself smiling. The idea of seducing Neon into a one-night stand was very, very tempting.

But did she have the courage to do it?

Chapter Three

They spent the afternoon on the beach, and Merle passed a pleasant few hours lazing under the shade of a beach umbrella, catching up with Bree, while the men surfed and played Frisbee and other sports on the sand as the sun dipped lower, the girls occasionally joining in or splashing in the shallows.

It was odd to think this wasn't a holiday for the majority of the group. They actually lived like this. The memory of the cold, wet weather she had left behind made her shudder. She couldn't imagine being exposed to this sort of life day in, day out. Would it get dull after a while? There would have been a time when she thought it would, as she loved her job. Lately, however, work had become a slog, and coping with the demanding needs of her mother had begun to weigh heavily on her shoulders. The thought of sacrificing university life to spend every weekend lying on the beach in the sun seemed very attractive.

"So?" Bree asked out of the blue.

"So what?" Merle had thought her sister was asleep as she hadn't spoken for a while. The younger girl looked over, shading her eyes with her arm.

"Have you thought any more about taking me up on my bet?"

"Are you still going on about that?"

"I saw the way you looked at him." Bree's eyes sparkled. "Am I in danger of losing my first fifty bucks?"

Merle sighed. "I doubt it. Do you really think I'm brave enough to suggest a one-night stand to someone like Neon?"

Bree smile turned into a curious frown. "What do you mean?"

"Well, look at him, and look at me. Mr. Surf Dude and Miss Prim and Proper? How likely would he be to say yes? Being turned down would be a horrific embarrassment."

"Turned down?" Bree started laughing again. "Have you looked in the mirror lately?"

"What's your point?"

"Merle, I wouldn't have suggested him if I didn't think he'd jump you at the first opportunity. I guarantee you, there's no way he'd turn you down."

Merle rolled her eyes. "Of course not, I'm breathing."

Bree smiled. "Actually he doesn't sleep with everything going. He can afford to be picky. And I'm telling you—you're gorgeous enough to catch his eye. I've seen the way he looks at you too, and you've only been here half a day."

Merle grew hot, or was it the unrelenting sun on her cheeks? "He told Jake I was puritanical."

"Well, you are." Bree grinned. "But even so, I've seen him staring at you. There's *no way* he's not interested in getting you into bed." She shrugged. "Anyway, he's a nice guy. He wouldn't hurt your feelings, even if he didn't fancy you. But I'm telling you, he does." She winked at Merle. "So, are we on?"

Merle glanced across at where the guys were now throwing a rugby ball to one another, seemingly unable to sit still for more than five minutes. She watched as Neon play-tackled one of the other guys to the ground. He was like essence of man.

How on earth could Bree think she would have the courage to tell him she was up for a one-night stand? She couldn't think how she'd even broach the topic, let alone go through with the act itself.

And yet... She felt a strange stirring in her stomach at the thought of walking up to this guy—this stranger, when she didn't even know his second name—and kissing him, letting him touch her in places she hadn't been touched for what seemed like an eternity.

It wasn't something English Merle would ever consider doing. But wasn't that the point? Here, thirteen thousand nautical miles away, she could be anyone she wanted. Kiwi Merle could have a completely different personality from what she normally had. Wasn't that an exciting thought?

She wasn't usually impetuous. But maybe Kiwi Merle was. Her heart thumped. "All right, it's a deal."

Bree stared at the hand Merle held out. She reached out and shook it, a smile creeping onto her face. "I didn't think you'd accept. Mind you, saying it's one thing—doing it's another."

"If it happens, I swear, you'll be the first to know."

The group of men came over, their rugby game finished. Shirtless again, wearing only swimming shorts, Neon grabbed a bottle of water and drank two-thirds of it in one go, then poured the remainder over his head, scattering them with drops as he shook it like a dog. Merle sighed.

"Sorry," he said. Beads of water trailed down his broad chest, and as he ran a hand through his hair, it sprang back up, scattering further droplets over her. She hadn't been complaining, but she didn't know how to explain that.

"No worries," she said, echoing his earlier words, trying to put on the Kiwi accent.

Neon laughed. "That was more Australian."

"Same thing, isn't it?"

He grinned at her mischievous smile. She was looking at him like she wanted to do a re-enactment of her ice lolly performance on him, and he remembered the way she'd stared at him when Jake first introduced them, her eyes like saucers. This English academic definitely had red blood running beneath the surface.

On impulse he said, "Want to go for a walk?"

She blinked. "Oh. Er, sure." She glanced at her sister, who grinned, amused. Merle turned her back on her and smiled at Neon. "Maybe you can tell me what some of those plants are growing along the beach."

Bree snorted.

He raised his eyebrows. "Less of the incredulousness, missy. I'm an expert on New Zealand botany, if you must know."

Merle let him pull her to her feet again and dusted herself. "Really?"

"Absolutely. That's a tree and that's a flower—what more do you want to know?" He smiled as they laughed, and he handed Merle her wide-brimmed hat. "Don't want you getting burned."

"Thanks."

Bree winked at her sister. "Have a nice nature trail." She lifted her hand as if to wave at Merle, but spread her fingers as if indicating the number five. Merle frowned at her, and Bree grinned and covered her face with her hat.

Merle stepped over Bree and scuffed sand over her before following him along the beach. Clearly they had been talking about something that embarrassed her. What was it?

Something to do with him?

The day was growing long, and some of the group had gone up to the beach house to light the barbecue for dinner. It was his favourite time of the day, the sun low on the horizon, the air humid and sultry. Merle's skin was a light pink in spite of the fact that she'd applied lotion several times during the day. She didn't say anything for a while as they walked, and neither did he. Their bodies seemed to be having a conversation of their own. He was very aware of her pale arm next to his, the glisten of moisture in the V of her breasts, and the sexy sway of her hips.

"I'm sorry for earlier," she said eventually.

"Hmm?"

"For insulting you, about Shakespeare. I didn't mean it. I'm not normally so rude."

He laughed. "No worries." But he appreciated the apology.

"Does this pattern mean anything?" She indicated the tattoo on his upper arm, her finger lightly tracing the black design. A shiver ran through him.

"Well, this is a koru—a curled-up silver fern. The fern's the symbol for New Zealand—you've probably seen it on the All Blacks' national rugby team shirt, and the Silver Ferns are the national netball team. You'll see the pattern everywhere here."

"Yes, I thought I'd seen it before." She looked up at him. She had beautiful dark blue eyes, but he found them difficult to read. What was she thinking? He picked up a flat stone and skimmed it into the ocean, conscious of her watching him.

She cleared her throat. "What are those beautiful trees with the red flowers? I've seen them everywhere."

"Pohutukawa." He led her over to them. "We call them our Christmas trees because they always flower at this time of year.

See—I do know something about plants." He smiled and she laughed, then repeated the word perfectly. He raised his eyebrows. "That's impressive—it usually takes people several goes to get that right."

"I have an ear for languages."

"Oh? Can you speak any others?" He ducked under an overhanging branch. A couple of the trees formed a natural nook by a cluster of rocks. He sat on one, and she perched across from him. Her sundress had a split at the bottom and it now parted, revealing her pale and shapely legs to mid-thigh. Her hands rested on the rock, and as she leaned forward, her breasts strained at the fabric, and he had a terrific view down her cleavage. Wow, she was hot. He blinked and tried to concentrate on her face.

"I'm fluent in French and German, and I can get by in Spanish and Italian. And I can insult you in several other languages."

He laughed. "Go on then."

She thought about it. "*Caesar si viveret, ad remum dareris.*"

"What does that mean?"

"It's Latin—it means 'If Caesar were alive, you'd be chained to an oar.'"

He burst out laughing. She smiled, studying him for a moment. He got the impression she was trying to decide something, but he couldn't guess what she was thinking.

He took off his sunglasses so he could see her better, putting them in his pocket. She blushed as he surveyed her, the same as she had when they first met, and he smiled again. She really was lovely. Her blue eyes were wide and serious. She swallowed, as if she was nervous, although he couldn't think what about.

Finally she gave a little, resigned sigh. *"Voulez vous coucher avec moi, ce soir?"*

He grinned. "Even if I hadn't heard the song, French happens to be one language I *am* familiar with."

She studied him, her face serious. Then, taking him completely by surprise, she said again, *"Voulez vous?"*

He stared at her. His eyebrows rose as he realised she wasn't just repeating the phrase, she was *asking him* if he wanted to sleep with her tonight.

He was completely stunned. Not because she'd been so forward, necessarily—there was nothing wrong with women taking the initiative, as far as he was concerned, and in fact he found it quite a turn-on normally. But that Merle should say something so blatant...

They studied each other for a moment. He felt baffled. Was she serious? It wouldn't be the first time he'd misunderstood the signs—every guy had a story like that, and once he'd even been slapped, although in his defence he'd only been fifteen at the time. But Merle certainly seemed serious.

He couldn't make her out at all. Her face was devoid of emotion, her eyes calm. Was this a regular thing for her? Did she sleep around a lot? Again, that didn't particularly bother him—he enjoyed sex, so why shouldn't women? But he couldn't think that was the case. Jake had said she wasn't impulsive, that there was no way she'd be interested in a holiday romance, and that she never went to bed with anyone without dating them for six months first. Was she really suggesting sex then? If so, how come she was so composed, so emotionless? He frowned, completely at a loss as to what to say.

He'd just started to formulate a reply in his head when he saw the pulse in her throat. It beat rapidly, and as he looked farther down, he saw her breasts rising and falling in rapid succession, in spite of her apparent lack of emotion. He glanced back at her face. Her eyes shone with panic. And then he understood.

She didn't do this all the time. In fact she'd probably never done it before in her life. Suddenly he doubted she'd had many partners at all. She was dedicated to her career, and that would mean little time for love or romance. But she'd travelled across the other side of the world for a little freedom from the ties of her everyday life, and she'd decided to take the opportunity to be adventurous, to step out of her comfort zone, desperate for some excitement, for hot but meaningless sex. And out of all the men in their group today, she'd chosen him.

In spite of the fact that he knew many women found him desirable, Neon felt flattered. It was a superficial attraction, sure—she'd made it clear she hadn't been drawn to his intellect. But he'd made her laugh several times that day, and anyway, what was wrong with straightforward physical attraction, in this setting anyway? She wasn't looking for a meaningful relationship. She was looking for fun.

And *that* he could understand.

Merle's mouth had gone dry. She'd expected him to jump at the offer of sex with no strings attached, but his frown made her realise there was more to him than she'd thought.

Oh great, I've picked a hot guy with principles. It had taken an immense amount of courage for her to say what she'd said, and now he was going to turn her down. She would have to walk back to the group rejected and excruciatingly embarrassed. What on earth must he think of her?

Panic overwhelming her, she opened her mouth to blurt out she'd been joking when his frown lifted, his lips curving in a smile. Relief flooded over her.

Standing, he moved closer to her and took her hands in his, pulling her toward him. She stood, toes sinking in the sand, heart thudding as he stroked her palms with his thumbs.

"You want to play with me?" he asked mischievously.

What a great way to put it. "Yes please," she said breathlessly.

He gave a little laugh, his eyes crinkling with affection and amusement. "How British! So polite."

She didn't know what she expected him to do next. She'd practically given him carte blanche to do anything he wanted, and wondered if he would grab her butt, or her breasts, and try to tune her in like Phil used to do, thinking it turned her on to have her nipples squeezed until she winced.

She didn't expect him to link her fingers with his, still by their sides, fix her with a gentle smile and lower his mouth to hers.

He kissed her softly, just a brush of lips, but it made her zing all over, an ice-cube running down her spine, her breasts and thighs tightening. Her heart pounded, but she made herself remain calm, though she knew her breath was coming quickly, and her nipples were standing through her dress like buttons.

He pulled back and looked at her. His brown eyes were warm as melted chocolate, full of smiles. "You know what a *hongi* is?"

"Is that the Māori greeting?"

He nodded. Leaning forward, he pressed his nose gently against hers. "When we *hongi*, we share the breath of life. You're not a *manuhiri* anymore—a visitor. You're *tangata whenua*. One of the people of this land."

"Oh." She blushed. "What a nice thing to say."

He chuckled. "A gift from me to you." He released her

fingers and stepped a bit closer, resting his hands on her hips. "And here's the same thing in *pakeha*—that's non-Māori." He lowered his lips again.

Merle rested her palms on his bare chest as they kissed. His skin was warm, dusted with a light coating of sand. He slid one hand onto the small of her back, pulling her gently toward him, pressing their hips together. She felt him against the flat of her stomach, hard as a rock, and sighed, her mouth opening under his. He inhaled in response and his tongue brushed hers, warm and soft. It was an incredibly erotic, slow kiss, with the sun warm on their skin and the rush of the waves in the background. She raised her arms around his neck, slipping a hand into his damp hair, pressing fully along him, her breasts touching his chest. He ran his hands up her rib cage, then slipped them around her back, tightening his arms around her. It was the nicest kiss she'd ever had, and she wanted it to go on forever, trying to capture the moment so she could replay it in the future when she returned to cold, wintry England.

When they eventually drew apart, they were both breathing heavily. He widened his eyes with the mischievous look she'd begun to realise was his default setting. "You're sexy as," he said, brushing her cheek with his hand.

"Sexy as what?"

He laughed. "That's what we say here. Sweet as. Hot as. Sexy as. All three of which you are." He glanced back at where the rest of their group were starting to pack up. "Time to go back." He looked at her. "I'm sleeping outside tonight—I've got a tent. It's small, but if you want to join me, you're very welcome."

"Really?"

He laughed again. "Absolutely. Only we'll have to keep our voices down—the tent is hardly soundproof and there's no lock. Think you can do that?" His eyes gleamed.

She felt breathless with anticipation. "I'll do my best." Heart thumping, she gave him a saucy look. "You'll have to cover my mouth if I cry out."

His eyes went hot. "Oh my." He grabbed her hand. "Come on, let's get dinner over with. I don't think I'm going to be able to wait."

The next few hours passed with agonising slowness. Merle picked at the barbecued fish and tried not to cast longing glances at Neon. He looked over at her occasionally, and every time he did, her heart pounded at the thought of the events to come.

In spite of her desperation for the time to pass, Merle had a great evening. With loud music on the radio, several bottles of wine being passed around and the Kiwis being such good company, she had an unusually good time being sociable for once.

She had a couple of glasses of wine to relax her but stopped then, wanting to make sure she wasn't incoherent when bedtime came. One of the guys tried to top up Neon's glass at one point and he shook his head. "I'm on day shift tomorrow. And I want to keep my wits about me." He cast a glance over at her and she shivered at the heat in his dark eyes.

Eventually people started yawning and everyone agreed it was bedtime. Bree took Merle into the beach house and showed her the sofa bed. "I've put you here. Hope that's okay."

"It's fine, thanks." Merle couldn't look at Neon. This was crazy. She'd gone stark raving mad.

Neon headed out with some of the others to the tents they had erected in the garden. "Good night," he called to those staying in the house. "My little blue tent is calling me."

Merle sat on the sofa bed and drew up her legs, aware that

he'd pointed out which tent was his for her benefit.

"Night, sis." Bree gave her a hug before disappearing into one of the two bedrooms with Jake.

Merle went into the bathroom, clutching her night-bag. She swallowed, studying her reflection in the mirror, her heart hammering. Was she brave enough to carry this through?

Chapter Four

Neon lay on top of his sleeping bag, staring up at the roof of his tent, just a couple of feet above his nose. It had been about half an hour since he'd left the house, and Merle hadn't appeared. He'd tried to read for a while but couldn't concentrate, every little sound making him tense. She wasn't going to come. Disappointment filtered through him. He'd really thought she wanted to. Clearly her nerves had won out. What a shame. He shifted irritably as a stone dug into his back. It was humid and stuffy in the tent, and he was so keyed up now, he'd have trouble getting to sleep. He wore only a T-shirt and boxers, but it was a warm night and he debated whether to take them both off.

Then, however, the tent rustled and he heard a zip opening. He pushed himself onto an elbow, looking at the entrance, and flicked on the small lamp by his sleeping bag, filling the tent with a warm glow. Her head appeared, her eyes wide in the semidarkness. "Sorry I'm late," she whispered. "Jake kept coming out for stuff." She got her shoulders in then stopped and looked around. "Christ, this is minute! Are you sure we'll both fit?"

"We'll have to squeeze up." He grinned, pleasure sweeping through him. He stifled a laugh at what she was wearing—if he'd needed any further confirmation that she didn't usually do this sort of thing, her pyjamas were enough to convince him. They were cotton and covered in pink bunnies.

She'd got stuck in the doorway, so he leaned forward and lifted her in, and she gave a small squeal, laughing as he zipped up the tent. He lay back, bringing her with him. She was right— it was incredibly small inside, but then it was supposed to be a one-man tent. Not a one-man, one-woman.

He turned on his side, propping his head with a hand. She did the same, facing him, just a few inches away. Her cheeks were flushed and she'd brushed her hair, and from the mintiness of her breath, her teeth as well. He felt a surprising surge of affection for her, though he hardly knew her at all. "I didn't think you were going to come."

"Well, I haven't *yet*." She rolled her eyes, then giggled.

He chuckled, reaching out to run a finger down her pink rabbit top. "Sexy." The smile broke out in spite of his attempts to hide it.

She looked at the pyjamas and back at him sheepishly. "I only brought two pairs with me and the other one is even worse. Neon—I didn't come to New Zealand planning this. I don't usually... I mean..."

"Hey." He frowned. "You don't have to justify yourself to me. You're over eighteen, right?"

She stared at him blankly.

"Merle, please tell me you're over eighteen."

She laughed. "I'm twenty-five, but thank you for the compliment."

"And you're single?"

"Yes."

"So am I—so we don't have to explain ourselves to anyone. What two consenting adults do in the privacy of their own...tent is nobody else's business."

She smiled. "You have a great attitude to life."

"It's got me into trouble a few times."

"I can imagine." She looked at her hands. "It's just...I don't want you to think I do this all the time. I'm not a hussy."

He grinned. "You think I'm insulted at your forwardness? Merle, you're young, you're beautiful, you're feeling horny and you chose me to help you out? Hey, I'm stoked!"

Merle couldn't help but laugh. Bree had been right—he *was* nice as well as hot.

She met his warm gaze and her heart thudded. What should she do now? Did he want her to take her clothes off? She was too nervous, plus she wasn't sure she had enough room to remove them.

He reached up and leaned over her, and for a moment, she thought he was going to kiss her. But he rummaged around in a bag at the end of the tent, and when she looked, she realised it was a small cooler. He extracted two plastic cups and a bottle of wine and held them up, raising his eyebrows. "Fancy a glass?"

She grinned. "I thought you were on duty tomorrow."

"Oh, I'll only have a splash. It's more to set the mood than anything."

He wanted to set the mood? She felt strangely touched. He wasn't just going to jump on her then. She took the cup he offered and held it up as he opened the bottle. There was so little room they had to manoeuvre around each other, making them both laugh.

"Cheers," he said once they'd tipped an inch into the two cups.

"*Skål!* That's Swedish."

"*Skål!*" They clunked cups and drank.

He looked at her, smiling. Her heart—which had been beating pretty rapidly all evening, increased in pace. His hair was ruffled and he had a scattering of sand on his arms. He was *gorgeous*. And he was looking at her as if she were covered in maple syrup and he wanted to lick it off. She couldn't believe her luck.

"Are we really going to have sex?" she said before she could stop herself.

He laughed and fixed her with a hot gaze. "Absolutely." He pointed to the tent zip. "I'm not letting you out of there until I've seen you naked." His eyes twinkled. "As endearing as those pyjamas are."

She poked her tongue out at him. "I may have to leave them on, anyway. I have no idea how I can possibly get undressed in here."

"I'm getting you out of those if I have to cut them off." He finished his wine and threw the cup in the cooler. "Okay that's it, I'm getting too hot." He grasped the back of his T-shirt and pulled it over his head. With no room to move his arms, however, he got stuck halfway and she had to help him out with the final pull.

Laughing, he ran a hand through his hair and then pulled her tight against him. He lowered his lips to hers, and electricity zapped through her from the base of her spine to the top of her head as she inhaled. It was nothing like the kiss on the beach. That had been slow, tentative and exploratory. Now she felt the full heat of his passion, the kiss searing her lips, his tongue hot and insistent, sweeping hers firmly. *Exhale, exhale, you can't breathe in continually or you'll hyperventilate.* But it was hard to catch her breath. She'd never been kissed like this in her life.

How could she compare this to the fumbling advances of Simon, or the wet, selfish kisses of Phil? That would be like trying to compare a four-course gourmet meal with school dinners.

Remembering something, she pulled back, placing a hand on his chest. "I forgot." She slipped her fingers in the pyjama pocket on her breast and pulled out a condom. "I thought we might need this. I stole it from Bree's purse."

He reached behind him and picked up another. "Hey, snap! I stole this from Jake." He winked at her. "Now we can do it twice!"

"Twice?" She felt slightly faint.

He looked at the pocket on her pyjamas where she'd extracted the condom and slipped a finger inside, wiggling it around. "You got anything else interesting in there?"

She giggled as he brushed her nipple. "No."

"Then time for these to come off." He pulled insistently at the pink bunnies.

Her mouth went dry, but he was already undoing the buttons. She watched as he undid them all and pulled the top off her shoulders. She blushed, starting to laugh as she ran out of space to move her arms. He had to help her tug it off, and by the end they were both laughing, hot and aroused in the tight space of the tent.

He threw the top to one side, and putting his arms around her, rolled onto his back, taking her with him.

"Wow." He cupped both her breasts, admiring her. "You are *so* sexy."

She smiled, breathless. "Thank you."

"You're very welcome, Miss I'm-So-Polite." He brushed her nipples with his thumbs and she sighed, lowering her head to kiss him. Lying full along him, she could feel him hard and ready for her. It was very warm in the tent and her chest stuck to his, which was so erotic the trousers of her pyjamas grew damp between her legs.

She giggled. "I'm sticking to you."

"Mmm." He didn't sound disappointed. "Are you hot?"

"It's very humid in here. I apologise if I pass out."

He laughed. He rolled to the right, lying beside her again, and raised himself on an elbow. His eyes were mischievous and she grew suddenly wary. He leaned over her and rummaged in the cooler again. When his hand came out, he held a rather wet ice cube, which he quickly popped in his mouth.

She looked up at him, puzzled. He raised a hand, asking her to wait. For a few moments he circled the cube in his mouth, then crunched it, his eyes sparkling with amusement.

He put his arms tight around her. Without warning, he bent his head and closed his mouth over her right nipple.

Merle squealed and braced her hands on his shoulders to push him away, but he was holding her so tight, it was like trying to push a brick wall, and she couldn't move. She gasped, tipping her head back, both nipples tightening so much it hurt. He sucked gently, his mouth gradually warming, and she caught her breath as his tongue circled like a warm sponge before he lifted his head to look at her, smiling.

"That was wicked!" she scolded, almost faint with desire.

He grinned. "Wicked's my middle name."

"You seem to have a lot of those."

"Eh?"

"Bree said your middle name was 'Feral'."

He laughed out loud and raised his eyebrows. "Like a savage, wild beast?"

"I think she meant more like a horny tomcat."

"Yeah, that about sums me up." He bent to kiss her but she pushed him away.

"Is it my turn with the ice now?" She looked at his boxers.

"Oh no. You've already had had your fun with me at the cafe, you little scamp. You got me so horny, I nearly came in my shorts like a sixteen-year-old."

"Oh..."

His eyes grew dark, and he brushed her lips with his. "Does that turn you on?"

She blushed, but said, "Everything's turning me on at the moment."

He chuckled, nibbling her ear. "I know what you mean—I made a mental list of all the things I wanted to do to you tonight, but I don't have enough self-control for half of them, sorry." He tugged at her pyjama bottoms. "Time to get these off, I'm getting desperate."

She was as well, and this time didn't hesitate to wriggle out of them. He pushed his boxers off and lay on his side, facing her. They admired each other's bodies for a moment, her heart beginning to pound again at the sight of him so ready for her.

"Nice," she whispered.

"Double nice."

He began to kiss her again, growing bolder, more insistent. His rising passion made her arch her back, pushing her breasts toward him, and she sighed as he played with her nipples, his fingers gentle but firm, his tongue warm on the sensitive skin.

After a while he trailed his hand along her abdomen, resting his fingers at the top of her pubic hair. She shivered as he traced a pattern on the flat of her stomach. He lifted his head momentarily and licked his fingers. He kissed her again as he slid his hand back down to her hair, then deeper, into the warm, moist part of her. She could have told him he wouldn't need any lubricant, and sure enough, as he found her slick and ready for him, he raised his head to look at her. She thought he would be smiling, but his eyes were hot, and he was obviously as desperate to be inside her as she was to have him inside.

"Mmm." He stroked her gently. "Triple nice."

She closed her eyes, sighing as his mouth closed over one nipple then the other, and it wasn't long before she caught his hand, unable to bear the torment any longer. "Now."

He retrieved one of the packets, tearing it open with his teeth. He put the condom on and lay on his back, pulling her on top of him, her long blonde hair falling across his chest like silk. She sat as upright as she could in the small tent and moved her hips, feeling the tip of him brush her swollen lips, which were so sensitive it made her gasp.

"You do it," he said huskily, cupping her breasts. "As slow as you want."

"No need for slowness." She pushed down in one firm movement, taking the whole of him inside, making both of them gasp out loud. He looked up at the tent roof, closing his eyes momentarily, trying to keep a tight hold on his self-control. She smiled wryly. Now she'd got rid of her reservations, she felt wildly uninhibited. She didn't want him in control. She wanted him as crazy as she felt.

She began to move on top of him, small movements initially, letting the tip of him slide inside her before lifting herself back up several times, then sinking down until he was completely sheathed in her, making him groan. She did this again and again, teasing him until he gave her a hot glare and, tightening his arms around her, rolled over carefully so she lay under him.

She gasped as he began to move more urgently, pulling her

against him so he could thrust more deeply inside her, angling himself so he aroused her as he moved. She had never made love like this. But of course this wasn't lovemaking—this was sex, pure, hard and simple, hot and erotic. She mustn't confuse the two.

He bent his head and kissed her, brushing his lips against her cheek and around to her left ear, his breath hot on her neck. "Come on, baby," he whispered, his hips moving rhythmically, insistently. "Come for me... I know you want to..."

Oh...she did. He was waiting for her, managing to hold back. But he didn't have long to wait. The orgasm built quickly, the muscles in her thighs and belly starting to tighten exquisitely. She gasped as the wave swept over her and everything began to pulse, and she knew she'd cried out, but she couldn't stop herself. His mouth closed over hers, muffling her moans, and some part of her brain thought about his comment on "the breath of life" and wondered if this was what it referred to.

She wrapped her legs around him and he groaned, plunging deeper into her, making her exclaim, then he tightened with his own climax and gave a deep shudder, his hips jerking, the muscles of his back rigid beneath her fingertips.

He lowered his head and rested it gently on her shoulder as their breathing began to quieten. Her heart pounded, and she could feel it echoed in his heartbeat against her chest. It was so hot in the tent they were drenched in sweat, and his hair curled damply around his forehead. When they moved, their skin peeled apart with a delicious sucking sound.

As she drifted back to earth, she waited for him to withdraw and roll over, but he didn't. Still inside her, he lifted his head and looked at her, his face lit with admiration and affection as he kissed her gently, touching his lips to her cheeks, her eyelids, then back to her mouth, soft butterfly kisses, tender and warm. "Did I hurt you?"

"No." Of all the idiotic things, and after everything they'd done, she blushed at the warmth in his eyes.

Luckily it was so warm in the tent he didn't notice. "Good. I'm sorry, I got carried away."

"I wanted you to."

"You are an incredibly hot woman." He moved his hips slightly against hers. "And the double meaning was intended." Smiling, he kissed her again. "I am so lucky. This was not how I envisaged my day ending when I woke up this morning."

She laughed. He withdrew from her slowly and rolled onto his back, sighing.

Merle pushed herself up and looked at him. He had one arm across his face, his breathing beginning to calm. He'd be asleep in seconds. Smiling, she reached for her pyjamas.

"Hey, where are you going?" He grabbed her wrist before she could pull on the pyjama bottoms.

"Back to my bed. Before anyone notices I've gone."

He gave her a reproachful look, reached to one side and found the other condom, then waved it at her. "We've got one left."

She laughed. "Really?"

"Well, I might need a few minutes."

She rolled her eyes. "You have to work tomorrow. You need your sleep and I can see you're tired. Go on, I don't mind. I got what I came for!"

He studied her, frowning. Then he released her hand but grabbed her long hair instead. Slowly he wound it around his fingers, tighter and tighter, until he forced her to move closer to him to avoid losing a handful.

"Ow."

"Well, do as you're told then."

"You can't tell me what to do just because we've had sex."

"Watch me." He tucked her under his right arm, and smiling, she curled against him, resting her head on his shoulder. She hadn't expected this. His hand stroked slowly down her back and he kissed the top of her head, a gesture that made her grow warm inside as well as out.

After a while, she lifted herself onto an elbow and looked at him, leaning on his chest. He watched her lazily, tracing patterns with his fingers on her hip.

She bent her head and licked in the hollow of his throat, tasting salt.

He sighed. "Mmm."

She smiled, sitting up. "I should go."

"After doing that?" He put his right hand on her back and pulled her toward him, catching her lips with his own.

"Neon..."

"Stop asking, I'm not letting you go."

"And stop ordering me around, *Napoleon...*"

"Right, that's it." He turned her onto her back and started kissing her again, moving her hands away when she tried to stop him, making her giggle and squeal as he traced his tongue lightly over her warm skin.

Playing with each other, they continued to grow hot and sticky, and their laughter echoed long into the night.

Chapter Five

Merle finally got to bed around two in the morning. Curling up in the sofa bed, a smile on her lips, she fell asleep instantly, exhausted from the remains of jet lag and her active evening. When she awoke, light flooded through the windows, and she could hear Bree and Jake talking, but nobody was up. She checked her watch—it had just gone eight.

She sat up and looked out of the window. Neon's tent had vanished. She knew his shift started at eight, so he had probably left a good hour earlier. She'd kept him up awfully late, considering he had to get up early. *Well, it was his fault.* She'd been prepared to leave after the first time. But he'd seemed as keen as her to make the most of their brief encounter.

She sighed and lay back, smiling. It had been such a fun evening, the best sex she'd ever had. It was a shame it was over, but at least she had some lovely memories to keep her warm.

She turned onto her right side and something scratched her arm beneath the covers. Lifting the duvet, she stared at the small bunch of wild flowers tied with a thin piece of flax that had been left there. She lifted them out, pressing them against her nose, inhaling the mild scent. He must have snuck in before he left and put them there. How sweet that he'd taken the time to pick them so early in the morning.

It was a good job she wasn't seeing him again. Mr. Feral would be a very difficult man to get over, should you fall for him. Now she understood why Ella had made such a fuss.

At that moment Bree's door opened and Merle covered the flowers, not wanting her sister to know about them, in spite of the fact that she had every intention of gloating over her recent sexual success.

"Morning." Bree walked across to the bathroom.

"Morning." Merle lay on her side, head propped on her hand, waiting for her sister to come out. When she did, Bree only had to take one look at Merle's face for the penny to drop.

"No! Last night?"

Merle held up both hands, showing her ten fingers. "That's a hundred bucks you owe me."

"Twice!" Bree burst out laughing and came and sat on the bed. "You're kidding me."

"Nope." Merle started giggling. "It was a bit of a squash in his tent though."

Bree stared at her, open mouthed. "I'm shocked."

"Well, it was your idea."

"I'm so pleased for you." She bent and hugged Merle, then drew back with eager eyes. "Tell me everything. Was he good?"

"Bree!"

"Come on, I want to know."

"I don't kiss and tell," Merle said primly. Then she laughed. "But he was *fantastic*. Thank you so much for introducing us."

"You are very welcome." Bree's eyes were mischievous. "But you've got three more to go to reach the golden three hundred dollars."

Merle rolled her eyes and fell back on the bed, laughing. "It took all my courage to ask Neon—I don't think I could do it again."

Bree shrugged. "I didn't say it had to be with five different men."

Merle sobered. "Oh no. I couldn't see him again. I..." Her voice tailed off. What was she trying to say? She thought about the flowers currently under the covers about two inches from Bree's butt. "I don't think that would be a good idea," she finished lamely. "I don't want to spoil it."

"Spoil it?"

Merle smiled. "I know what sort of a man he is. A real heartbreaker, if ever I saw one. It was great fun and I enjoyed myself, but I'm content with the treat I've had."

Bree's eyes softened. "I understand. I'm glad you had a good time." She kissed Merle's forehead. "Now, are you able to get up, or are you going to walk like you've been horse-riding for a fortnight?"

Merle pushed her off the bed. "Don't embarrass me. Go and tell your husband he has to make me breakfast."

Bree went off, laughing. Merle lay back and her hand crept under the covers to find the flowers. Thank goodness she wouldn't see him again. Because she could very easily fall in love with him, and that most definitely would not end well.

The next day, Bree had planned them so much to do, Merle thought she wouldn't have time to think about her wild night with Neon. However, it surprised her how often he crept into her thoughts. While walking around the Te Waimate Mission House, or watching the water tumbling at Rainbow Falls, the thought of him kissing her and the memory of his sandy skin under her fingertips kept popping into her head. Each time, it made her shiver, her cheeks flushing as she thought of how bold she'd been.

That night when she finally got to bed at Bree and Jake's house in Kerikeri, she lay there listening to the kiwi birds crying in the bush. She thought of his mischievous brown eyes and the way he'd been so gentle with her, and her mood gradually started to sour.

For as much as she'd enjoyed herself—and she had, very, very much—part of her had begun to wonder if sleeping with him had been the best idea. Now she couldn't rid herself of the thought of what it would be like to be married to a man who made her feel like that every day of every year. Imagine going to bed and being able to have sex like that as often as you liked. The thought made her tingle all over, and she cursed as she realised she would now judge every man she met against him and probably find them wanting.

No, that couldn't be the case. He was far from perfect. Yes he was gorgeous, but there was no way he was marriage material. She'd slept with him out of a purely physical need, and she had to keep reminding herself of that fact.

Her ideal man would be as good looking as Neon Carter but would also be interested in the same things as her and wouldn't be commitment-phobic—a man who would play with her at night and also entertain her during the day with his mind as well as his body.

However, as she dozed off to sleep, thinking about this mysterious man, he looked surprisingly like the rugby-playing, surfing firefighter she'd had such fun with the night before.

The following day was Christmas Eve, and during the day,

Merle went shopping in town with Bree, buying tree presents for the kids who were going to be at the party Jake's parents were having that afternoon.

"Are you sure they don't mind me coming?" she asked when they stopped for a quick coffee and a bite to eat in one of the many cafes in Bree's beautiful, tropical town. "I haven't had a proper invite." She sipped her latte, admiring the silver fern the barista had managed to create in the foam of milk on the top. It made her think of the koru in Neon's tattoo, and she gave a small sigh, trying to concentrate on what Bree was saying.

"We don't do invites in New Zealand." Bree laughed. "Honestly, Merle, it's so informal here. People are always turning up out of the blue. And anyway, it's not like a sit-down do or anything, it's only a barbie. Mum would be horrified." She grinned. Merle smiled, but there was an underlying tinge of sadness beneath it, and Bree sobered. "Crap, I shouldn't have mentioned Mum. How was she this morning?"

"Okay." Merle didn't want to spoil her sister's Christmas Eve. Susan had been tearful and aggressive on the phone, laying on the guilt about being lonely and left on her own. Merle knew her mother had been invited around to her uncle's house and would love being with all his children and grandchildren, but she still felt bad.

She'd wanted to cry at the anger and fear tarnishing her mother's voice. Merle knew Susan loved her and Bree. She tried to tell herself that when Susan said such terrible, hurtful things, it was the after-effects of the illness talking, not her, but deep down, Merle knew her mother had been like this before she grew ill. She'd always been manipulative, even when the girls were younger—it was just now she had a convenient excuse to hide behind.

Then guilt flooded her. Susan's insistence that she was still sick, that they hadn't got all the cancer, meant it was still possible the illness was dictating her behaviour. The doctors had insisted she was clear, but Merle was beginning to wonder whether her mother's claims that she could almost feel the disease clawing its way through her were just dramatic license intended to make her feel guilty or actually the truth. Might that explain why she was so cruel, so ravaged by fear and hurt?

It hadn't helped that Bree had run out to the shops, and Susan had been convinced her daughter was avoiding her. Which was possibly true. Susan had asked how Bree was, hoping, Merle knew, she would say Bree appeared lonely and desperate to come home.

She'd been unable to lie, knowing if she did so, it would only drag out the misery. "Bree's fine, Mum," she'd said. "She loves it here and she's happy. I'm sorry." The irony of apologising for her sister's happiness hadn't escaped her, but Susan didn't notice and burst into tears, and Merle spent an exhausting half an hour trying to comfort her. But at least the phone call was done for the day and she'd promised she would ring in the evening on their Boxing Day, and she would make sure Bree was there this time. She'd have to bully Bree to the phone. Bree didn't feel half as much guilt as she did, and always got exasperated when she knew her mother was demanding to talk to her.

Finishing their coffee and muffins, they went back to Bree's house to get ready for the party. Merle looked through her clothes, wondering what to wear. It was a lot warmer in the Northland than she'd expected, and the T-shirts she'd brought seemed too warm in the sultry, humid weather. Eventually she chose a dark pink camisole and a beautiful, long multicolour skirt she adored but was also cool. It was too hot for underwear, and she left off her bra and panties. Luckily Neon wasn't going to be there, or Lord knew what he would think.

Bree had already assured her he was going to his folks' for Christmas Eve.

They arrived at around six at Jake's parents' house, a stunning four-bedroom house in the middle of nowhere, or so it seemed to Merle, used to terraced and semidetached houses with about an inch of garden, where you could hear the neighbours shouting or having sex through the walls. Several acres of paddocks and bamboo trees surrounded the house, with bush to the south, and the only sounds she could hear were the tuis in the trees and the rush of the river at the bottom.

Jake introduced her to his parents and the rest of his family. Everyone was friendly and laid back. Merle wandered through the spacious living room and out the large sliding doors to the deck, humming to the Christmas songs playing. How wonderful to live in a place like this. A couple of bright-coloured parrots Bree had told her were called rosellas flew past her into the bush. She loved England, but there was something special about this country. She could see why Bree had fallen in love with it.

She paused on the deck. There were more people outside, relaxing on the loungers, some playing with the kids on the lawn, others working on the smoking barbecue. A few looked over and nodded hello, and she smiled.

Her gaze alighted on a figure lying on one of the loungers, and her heart seemed to shudder to a stop. She stared at Neon, who lay stretched out with his hands behind his head, wearing dark glasses and a brilliantly white short-sleeved shirt that made him look incredibly tanned, with dark blue shorts, barefoot as usual. Of course she couldn't see what he was looking at with his sunglasses on. Had he seen her? She turned and went straight back inside, heart pounding, walking through the house until she found Bree.

"You told me he wouldn't be here."

Bree studied her. Clearly she knew exactly who Merle was referring to. "I lied. Now chill out and go and get a drink."

Merle glared at her, but Bree walked off to talk to Jake's mum. Merle went over to the table where bottles of wine, beers and an assortment of alcohol-free drinks were scattered and started pouring herself a glass of Sauvignon. *Shit, shit, shit.* Her hand shook, slopping some of the wine over the side. Damn Bree and her stupid bet.

She felt a presence behind her and closed her eyes, not looking around, knowing who it was likely to be.

"Why don't you let me do that for you?" His deep voice sounded amused. He took the bottle from her hand. "Seems a shame to waste it." She heaved a sigh as he pressed against her back, leaning over to pour the rest of the glass. His voice, when he spoke again, was very close to her ear. "Well, look at you, Merle Cameron, blushing like a sixteen-year-old virgin. Aren't you delightful?"

Her cheeks burned. He filled the glass and placed the bottle on the table, but he didn't pull away. His hand rested on her hip.

She turned her head slightly but couldn't look up at him. "Hello, Neon."

"Hello, sweetheart."

Her face was so hot she knew her cheeks were scarlet. Her body tingled where he pressed against her at her shoulder and hip. *Best to address the issue immediately and then move on.* "I didn't get to say thank you, by the way...for the other night. And for the flowers. They were very...thoughtful."

"How very British, so polite." He nuzzled her ear. "You're very welcome. It was my...pleasure." He dropped a kiss on her shoulder, sending a hot rush through her.

Behind them, Jake said, "Come on you two, get a room."

Neon laughed, and she turned and glared at them both before picking up her glass and walking away. This was bad, bad news. She knocked back half the wine in one go. How on earth would she make it through the evening with him watching her with those gorgeous, hot brown eyes?

Jake winked at Neon. "I can't believe it. Looks like the ice queen's finally thawed. Am I about to lose our bet?"

Neon twisted the top off a beer and grinned. "I'm working on it."

"Bree told me what happened at the beach. You lucky bastard. Don't know how you manage it."

"Neither do I, in this case." Neon took a swig from the bottle. "I told you I wouldn't make a move on her. It was her suggestion."

Jake's eyes nearly rose off the top of his forehead. "You're shitting me."

"I shit you not."

"Jeez... Bree said she'd bet Merle she wouldn't have sex while on holiday, but I'd assumed you'd had to talk her into it."

Neon stared at him. "Bree said what?"

Jake carried on, oblivious to the way Neon's smile had faded. "She was talking to Merle about the fact that Merle hadn't had sex for ages, and Bree bet her she wouldn't be brave enough to ask a guy for a one-night stand. Bree was stunned Merle had the courage to go through with it."

Neon stared after Merle. She stood in the doorway to the decking, silhouetted by the sun. Once again her skirt was semitransparent and he could see the shape of her long legs. He could remember how it had felt to have them wrapped around him.

So, she had asked him to bed her because of a bet? He felt strangely insulted. And yet, what difference did it make? Bree had only given her a gentle push—she wouldn't have done it if she didn't want to. Though she hadn't mentioned Bree's part in it, it wasn't as if she'd slept with him out of false pretences. She'd been quite willing to leave after the first time and had made no show of demanding to see him again afterward. She'd been quite clear she wanted a bit of fun and nothing more.

And let's not be so hypocritical. He had made the bet with Jake, after all, even if it had been in jest.

Still, he felt annoyed at being manipulated. He wasn't quite sure how he had been, but he felt certain it had happened. So, she thought she controlled this situation? Well, he had something to say about that.

He sipped his beer. She stood slightly turned toward him and he could see the shape of her soft breasts beneath the pink top. Clearly she wasn't wearing a bra, and he was pretty sure she wasn't wearing panties either. Damn, now he had a hard-on. Perhaps she was more in control than he thought.

He walked up to her in the doorway. She glanced up as he paused, stepping aside to let him pass, her back up against the edge of the sliding door, but he didn't continue. Instead he moved closer until he was an inch away, looking down at her. Her eyes were the colour of a Kiwi summer sky. Her soft mouth was slightly parted, and her tongue moistened her lips as he looked at them.

Lowering his head before she could move away, he kissed her. He kept one hand in his pocket, and the other held his beer bottle—the only place they touched was their lips. Once he knew she wasn't going to move, he made it a long, leisurely kiss, stroking her tongue with his, enjoying the taste of her. It did nothing to help the problem in his shorts, but at that moment he didn't care.

Behind them, someone whistled and then everyone cheered.

Neon lifted his head, casting his family an amused glance before looking back at her. Her cheeks had flushed again, and she looked up at him, blinking a few times.

"What was that for?" She sounded breathless. He looked up, and she followed his gaze, seeing the bunch of mistletoe nailed above the door.

"Merry Christmas." He lowered his shades and took a swig from his beer, walking back to his lounger. Stretching out, he watched her stare at him. He blew her a kiss. Slowly, her lips curled. She looked gorgeous standing there, blonde hair lifting in the summer breeze, and suddenly he was very aware he was interested in more than a one-night stand.

Chapter Six

The evening grew long as the sun gradually set, and Jake's mum brought out some citronella candles and lamps to keep the insects away, bathing the decking in a yellow glow. The warm, humid air made Merle's hair stick to the back of her neck, and her skin was damp with perspiration.

Neon had kept his distance since he'd kissed her, choosing a seat across the other side of the decking when the barbecue was ready and not approaching her, even when he walked inside to get another drink.

Unfortunately, it didn't help Merle at all. She was as acutely conscious of him as if they were attached by a piece of electric cable. Every time he moved, or said something, or laughed—which he did a lot—she felt as if a thousand volts had passed along the cable between them. Eventually she sat back in her chair, brooding as she listened to him relating anecdotes to the members of his family sitting around him, causing everyone to laugh frequently at his amusing tales. He was funny and smarter than she had given him credit for—he had to be or he wouldn't have such a sharp wit and the ability to give such a quick retort.

She drank steadily as the evening progressed, knowing she was getting tipsy but finding it the only way to cope with her increasing agitation as the night wore on. Why the hell wasn't he just a meathead? Why did he have to be all suave and charming and funny? And why on earth had she slept with him? Now she couldn't get the thought of him kissing her out of her head. And the way he had thrust so deep inside her... *Oh dear God...*the thought made her grow wet between her thighs and that was *not* good news when she wasn't wearing any underwear.

Jake now teased Neon about his work, and she remembered he'd been on shift that day. "No, no, Neon's job is very important," Jake protested to everyone around them. "I'm telling you, when the one fire in a gazillion years happens in this town, the phone call will wake him right up in his office and he'll be raring to go."

Everyone laughed. Neon gave him a reproachful look, pointing a finger at him. "Now I'll have you know there are cats around here that would still be stuck up trees if it wasn't for me."

Something about his self-deprecating manner blew Merle's mind. Lust swept through her like a tsunami, roaring through her veins. She was so hot for him she was going to supernova.

At that moment he looked over at her as he sipped his beer, and electricity fired through her as sure as if he'd scuffed his feet on a carpet and touched his finger to her damp skin.

Cursing, she got to her feet and went inside, carrying her wineglass. She shouldn't drink any more, but she was desperate to stop the fire rushing through her veins and maybe, if she drank enough, she'd be too numb to feel anything.

She poured herself some wine, smiling as the woman next to her held out her glass, gesturing for Merle to fill hers up too.

"There you go." Merle finished off the bottle.

"Thanks." The woman smiled. She was in her early fifties, slender and beautiful, her brown hair peppered with grey and cut into a neat bob. "You must be Merle."

"Yes, that's right." Merle shook the other woman's hand as it was offered. "I'm sorry, you are...?"

"I'm Julia. It's very nice to meet you."

"You too," said Merle, wondering who she was.

"I've heard a lot about you."

"Oh?" Merle raised an eyebrow, smiling. "Good things I hope."

Julia gave a small laugh. "Oh yes." She didn't elaborate, but her eyes smiled, crinkling at the edges as she sipped her wine.

"And what are you two talking about?" Neon walked up to the table and poured himself a Coke.

"Nothing." Julia's face was the picture of innocence. Merle looked from her to him and back again. The two of them were staring at each other, some message passing between them, although it remained unspoken. Neon gave Julia a glare followed by a slight shake of his head. She tipped hers in reply, her eyes dancing.

"Go away." He turned Julia around and pushed her toward the garden. Laughing, she acquiesced, casting a last look over her shoulder, winking at him.

Merle raised an eyebrow. "That wasn't very polite."

He shot an exasperated look in Julia's direction, then looked back at Merle and sipped his Coke, his other hand on his hip. "She's got a naughty streak—I was avoiding disaster."

Merle stared at him, puzzled. "What's going on?"

He finally realised she didn't know who Julia was and sighed, pointing with the hand holding the glass toward the older woman. "That's my mum."

"Your mum? Oh shit!" Eyes wide, Merle clapped a hand

over her mouth, laughing. "How the hell did she know who I was?"

He looked uncomfortable. "I might have mentioned something about meeting a hot girl the other night. I guess Jake filled her in on the rest."

"Oh for the love of... She's going to think I'm a right hussy."

He started to smile. "Well, if the wide-brimmed hat fits..."

She glared at him but couldn't stop a smile creeping onto her face. She had taken off her shoes and now, in spite of the fact that she was tall for a woman, he towered over her, taking her breath away. There were very few men around who could make her feel small, but he definitely fit into that category.

He glanced at her breasts, which were outlined nicely by the tight pink top, the nipples standing out like embroidery on the cloth. She didn't try to cover herself, but bravely let him look, waiting for his gaze to come back to hers, which it did eventually, his eyes warm and lit with the mischievous look she was beginning to know and love.

For a long moment they studied each other. Desire swept through Neon, which was unsurprising as he'd been watching her all evening, unable to stop thinking about their night in the tent. That evening had imprinted itself on his mind. He'd been captivated by her luscious curves and her incredible sense of fun that had kept him laughing all night, until she finally drove him to the point where his body had taken over. She'd enjoyed sex more than any woman he'd ever been with, and he'd been with a few. Maybe it had been because she hadn't expected to see him again, and it was easier to be open and abandoned with a stranger. Would it be that way if they had sex again?

As he looked at her, he wondered what was going on behind her cool blue eyes. He could tell from the way her body reacted to him that she wanted him, but he was well aware your body and your mind could desire two completely different things. However, the urge to drag her off somewhere and re-enact their previous encounter crowded his mind like too many people trying to get into a lift, and he was going to have to act on it, even if it meant getting shot down in flames.

He glanced over at his family sitting outside. Actually he hadn't mentioned to his mother exactly what had happened at the beach, although he'd admitted to her on the following day he'd met a girl he liked. She'd put two and two together, knowing her son well enough, and had teased him about his ability to charm women on first sight. She'd then been intrigued by his offhand comment that Merle was "special". Seeing the light in her eyes, he'd immediately tried to correct himself, but had been too late to stop her being interested and then had to endure half an hour of grilling as to exactly why he'd found this English girl so entrancing. Unable to answer her, he'd eventually lost his temper and stormed out, but she'd merely seemed to take that as a sign that this Merle had somehow got to him in a way no other woman had lately.

Shaking his head, determined not to get dragged into such womanly scheming, he noted currently he and Merle were the only ones inside the house, and nobody seemed to have noticed they were missing. He looked back at Merle. She sipped her wine, her eyes gleaming, a small smile curving her lips behind the glass.

He cleared his throat. "Would you like to...maybe..."

"Oh, thank God." She put her glass on the table. "I thought you'd never ask."

Laughing, feeling a surge of pleasure, he grabbed her hand and led her across the room, heading for the bedrooms at the far end of the house. She followed him on light footsteps, her laughter echoing behind him, and he grinned as he pulled her into the right-hand bedroom, closing the door behind them. He went to lock the door, only to realise it had no lock.

"Shit."

She glanced over her shoulder, saw the en suite bathroom in the corner and headed over to it, taking him with her.

"Merle…"

She pulled him inside and shut the door, twisting the button and locking it. When she turned around, her eyes were alight with amusement.

"Are you serious?" He glanced around. It was a nice bathroom, fairly large, and he rather liked the tiling, but it was still a bathroom, not the most romantic of settings he would have chosen. "Here?"

She began undoing his shirt buttons. "I'm so aroused I was close to doing you in the living room. Get your clothes off, Carter." Releasing the last button, she pushed the shirt off his shoulders. "We're going to have to be quick."

"Speed is not a problem, believe me."

She started laughing, and he joined in, letting his shirt drop to the floor, desire making him hard as a rock. He pulled her to him and nuzzled her ear. "Are you drunk?"

She ran her hands up his chest, sighing as her fingers brushed his defined muscles. "I might have had a couple of glasses. God, you've got an incredible body."

"I don't know that this is such a good idea…" He didn't stop kissing her neck, though. Her compliment pleased him, made him glow a little.

"What are you talking about?" She pressed her hips against him and looked up, her eyes hot. "I can tell you want me."

"Well, duh. But I don't like the idea of taking advantage of you like this."

She pulled back and frowned at him. "Jeez, you sound practically Victorian. Neon, I'm not hammered, if that's what you're thinking. I know perfectly well what I'm doing."

"Okay, you've convinced me." He wanted her so badly he didn't think he could have stopped even if she'd wanted him to.

She gave an exultant laugh and slid her arms around him. "Good."

He pushed her back until her legs met the hand basin, kissing her hot and hard, running his hands over her breasts. She went to pull off her top, but he stopped her. "No don't. You're all soft like this..." Her breasts were heavy in his hands, and his fingers slid over the fabric easily as he brushed his thumbs across her nipples.

"You're not." The words came out breathless as she moved her hips against his.

"The perfect combination." He started to hitch up her long skirt. When it got to her knees he ran a hand up the outside of her thigh, reaching around to cup her ass.

"Whoa." He pulled back and stared at her as his hand found only skin.

"What?" She grinned. "I was hot."

"Oh God, you're telling me." He lifted her skirt up so he could cup both cheeks with his hands.

Merle rested back on the hand basin and shot up again with a squeal. "Jeez, that's cold!"

He laughed and moved her to the side, kicking the laundry basket away to make room. She met the wall with a bump and gasped, pulling his head down, kissing him deeply, opening her mouth to accept his tongue, matching it stroke for stroke with her own.

Sighing, he pushed a knee in between her legs, nudging them apart, then slipped a hand beneath her skirt. He knew better than to worry about lubrication this time and, sure enough, as he brushed his fingers through her hair, he found the warm folds of her skin already slick with moisture, his fingers sliding easily.

He gave a half laugh, half groan. "God, you're sexy." She laughed and he kissed her as he stroked her, slipping two fingers inside, sighing at the wetness and the heat of her.

She pushed his hand away, however, fumbling at his shorts. "No time for that. Come on, I want you inside me." She stopped, staring at him. "Oh crap, I forgot..."

Grinning, he pulled back, putting a hand in his pocket and drawing out a condom.

She looked up, raising an eyebrow. "You came prepared?"

"I knew you were going to be here tonight."

Her eyes widened. "You assumed I'd have sex with you again? That's a big assumption, mister."

Uh-oh. He shrugged. "Hoped, not assumed."

She studied him for a moment. He could see her deciding whether or not she should be insulted. Clearly she then realised how ridiculous that would be and grinned. "Fair enough."

He laughed, relieved, and tore open the packet, pulling down his shorts a little, sliding the condom on. She lifted a leg around him, moving herself into position, but she wasn't quite where he wanted her.

Placing both hands beneath her backside, he lifted her, wrapping both her legs around his waist. She squealed, flinging out an arm for balance, knocking several bottles off the nearby shelf as she did so. He laughed. "Don't worry, I've got you."

"Neon!" She clutched hold of him. "I'm heavy—you'll drop

me!"

He looked at her wryly. "Sweetheart, I have to be able to lift a hundred and five kilos, and I can do almost double that. I don't think you weigh *quite* that much."

She stared at him, wide-eyed. "I keep forgetting you're a firefighter. Wow." She ran her fingers up the tight muscles of his arms, her eyes glinting. "Can I slide down your pole please?"

He chuckled. "Absolutely, but stop making me laugh or we won't get anywhere." He pressed her against the wall, his arms tight around her, pushing the tip of himself into her warmth. "Now relax." He kissed her deeply, waiting until she felt safe enough to let go of the tight grip she had around his neck, her thighs slackening. Slowly he lowered her, sliding right into her warm velvet skin until she was completely impaled on him.

"Oh my." Her pupils were so dilated her eyes looked black. She linked her ankles behind his back, slipping her hands through his hair, which was damp with sweat. She pulled his head forward and he kissed her again as he began to move, starting slowly, worried about hurting her, but after a while, she tightened her legs around him as he pushed forward, encouraging him to deepen his thrusts. Before long, he was past thinking, past caring, driven by instinct and a desperate hunger for this wild and beautiful woman.

"Oh God...oh God...oh God..." she started to say each time as he thrust even harder, making him smile in spite of his rising passion.

"Don't make me laugh."

"I...can't...help it..." She tipped her head back. "It feels like...you're trying to...spear me...through the wall!"

"Do you want me to stop?" *Please, please don't say yes.*

"It's...too late...for that..." She panted, unable to kiss him now, to do anything but breathe in big gasps. Her eyes drifted shut. "I think I'm...going to...oh!"

Her muscles tightened around him, squeezing him as her orgasm started. "Open your eyes," he demanded, and she did so, blinking as she tried to focus on him, small cries escaping her soft, bruised mouth. At that moment, her head tipped back on the wall, her eyes wide with pleasure, he'd never seen anything so beautiful and erotic.

It was too much for him and his own climax started, his muscles pulsing as he felt the familiar rush and focus of his whole being in his groin.

At that exact moment, just as they reached their peak, someone knocked at the door.

Chapter Seven

They both jumped but were too far gone to stop, and Merle clapped a hand over her mouth, trying to cover up her cries, while Neon leaned his head on her shoulder, cursing and laughing at the same time as his body continued to pulse.

"What?" he barked out as soon as he was able, hoping fervently it wasn't his mother.

"Are you all right in there?" Jake's concerned voice was followed by a muffled snort, presumably from Bree. "It sounds like you're in pain!"

"Oh Christ." Merle met Neon's gaze, trying hard not to laugh and failing miserably.

He glared at the door. "Fuck off, Jake!"

His cousin's laughter echoed and Neon shook his head, joining in, planting a kiss on Merle's hair as his body finally began to calm. "I'm so sorry!"

"I'm not—I haven't had so much fun in years." She met his eyes, her own very warm and filled with amusement as her breathing started to slow. "Oh my God, I swear I'm not going to be able to walk for a week." She unlinked her ankles and he let her slide down him as he withdrew carefully. She groaned as she straightened her legs, wincing.

Laughing ruefully, he pulled his shorts up then wrapped

her in his arms. She lifted her head and he studied her, smiling, bending to kiss her, long and languidly, tightening his arms around her. Afterward he rested his cheek on the top of her head, kissing her hair as she snuggled up to him.

It took a moment for him to move, but eventually he said, "We'd better go out. I think they're still out there." He bent and picked up his shirt, pulling it on and buttoning it.

"Can you go first? I need to...you know." She nodded at the toilet.

"Of course." He unlocked the door. He looked over his shoulder, then came back and pressed a kiss to her lips. He hesitated.

"Go on." She smiled. "I'm okay."

He met her gaze. For a second he saw a hint of sadness in her eyes, like the glimpse of a coin at the bottom of a well. Then it vanished and she winked, playful once again.

Blowing her a kiss, he went out and shut the door behind him.

Merle waited for a moment. There was a second of silence, then Bree and Jake burst out laughing.

"Very funny," Neon said wryly. "Bastard."

"Neon, we could hear the two of you from down the hall, it was hardly a secret assignation."

Merle groaned quietly.

"So what? She was giving me an early Christmas present."

"Oh, she was giving you one all right."

A string of expletives came from the firefighter, followed by more laughter from the other two.

"Where's Merle?" Amusement filled Bree's voice.

"Waiting for you two to bugger off. Come on, leave her alone and don't embarrass her—she gets enough of that from me." His voice grew fainter as he propelled them out of the room.

Merle sat with her face in her hands. Dear God, what was she doing? She was a guest in a strange house and she'd dragged a man off for a quickie while his mother was in the next room, for crying out loud. *Oh please, God, don't let Julia have heard us.*

It was no good—she couldn't stay in there all night. She had to go out at some point.

She checked herself in the mirror. Her hair was ruffled, her cheeks were flushed, her lipstick had vanished and her lips were swollen. She looked like she'd had sex. Funny that. She looked away, wincing. Hopefully it would be dark enough so nobody would notice.

She unlocked the door and opened it. She walked out, stopping immediately. Neon stood in the doorway to the bedroom, leaning on the doorframe, arms crossed. As she came out, he gave a small laugh. "I was beginning to think you'd set up camp in there."

"I thought about it." She blushed at the memory of what they'd done.

He smiled as her cheeks reddened. "You're the only woman I've known who blushes *after* sex." He held out a hand toward her. "Come on, tiger. Bree and Jake are ready to go."

Oh, thank God. Maybe they'd be able to sneak out without seeing anyone. She slipped her hand into his, her heart thumping as she thought of where the fingers grasping hers had just been. She had to stop doing this. She didn't have the constitution to withstand the embarrassment afterward.

They walked down the hall and into the living room, and to her horror, she realised everyone had moved inside. Luckily, though, nobody else—apart from Jake and Bree, who were giggling like five-year-olds—had noticed they were missing.

"I'd better say goodbye to Jake's parents."

"I'll get your sandals." He headed for the decking.

She thanked Jake's mum and dad for inviting her to their party and promised she'd be back the following day for Christmas dinner.

When she turned around, Julia stood there waiting to say goodbye, clutching the hand of the tall, grey-haired man who had been talking to Neon earlier that evening. *Oh no, surely not.*

Julia smiled, eyes sparkling. "Goodbye, Merle." She came forward to give her a kiss on the cheek. "This is my husband, Pierre, by the way."

"Ah," said Merle, interested even though she'd blushed furiously. "So that's where he got his name!"

Pierre laughed, taking her hand and kissing the tips of her fingers. "And he has never forgiven me for it!" His accent was a strange blend of Kiwi and French, and his gesture showed his European heritage.

She smiled, speaking to him in French. "Are you interested in history?"

He nodded, his eyes widening at her fluency. "I'm a secondary school history teacher."

"Oh! I'm a lecturer in medieval history at the University of Exeter." Merle didn't miss the way Julia elbowed her husband in the ribs, and his answering squeeze of Julia's hand.

"Wonderful!" said Pierre enthusiastically. "Do you cover any French history?"

"Well, Crécy, Poitiers and Agincourt, obviously," she teased, referring to the three great English victories of the Hundred Years' War.

He laughed. "So where did you meet Neon?"

Merle opened her mouth, but their son was already walking back up to them, Merle's sandals in his hand, and he fixed his parents with a reproachful stare. "Okay, folks, show's over." He caught Merle's hand and backed away, pulling her toward the front door.

"Nice to meet you," she said over her shoulder as Julia reached up to whisper something in her husband's ear. Pierre nodded, looking back at Merle, smiling.

Neon looked exasperated. Merle's good humour faded. He didn't want her talking to them. Well why would he? It wasn't as if she were his girlfriend or anything. She was only a holiday fling.

"Sorry," he said.

"For what?"

"Well, I doubt you expected the third degree from my parents when you made that offer on the beach."

She started to smile. "No, I suppose not."

He led her out into the drive, pulling her to one side. "Merry Christmas." He gave her a last kiss.

"Merry Christmas," she said when he raised his head. His kiss lingered on her lips like a snowflake.

"Have a great day tomorrow. I doubt it'll be turkey and roast potatoes."

She laughed. "I must admit, I've never had a barbecue on Christmas Day! But there's a first time for everything."

"There certainly is." He smiled.

"Are you spending the day at your parents'?"

"Most of it. I'm on nights for the next two days."

"On Christmas Day!"

He grinned. "Someone has to man the fort. It can be busy. There's often a lot of car accidents, drunk driving, you know."

She nodded. When she thought of firefighters, she always thought about them fighting fires and forgot they did other stuff. "Well, be careful," she said awkwardly.

"I will." He smiled, his eyes warm.

She hesitated. She couldn't think of anything to say except, "See you." What did you say to someone you'd just had wild, passionate sex with, but who you were probably never going to see again?

"See you."

She walked over to the car. Bree and Jake were already inside and she climbed in the back. Jake pulled away smoothly.

She looked at her hands, then out the window. Eventually, however, she had to look at Bree and Jake. Jake was glancing at her in his rear-view mirror with an amused expression on his face, and Bree turned around to look at her over the headrest, eyes brimming with delight. Merle met her gaze and glared.

They both burst out laughing. Merle studied them. "Ha-ha, very funny. This is all your fault, Bree Warren."

"Don't know what you're fed up about. Sounded like you were having a good time to me."

Merle blushed scarlet and Bree reached over and grasped her hand. "I'm sorry, I shouldn't tease. I'm very happy for you. And you've earned yourself another fifty bucks, anyway!"

Two more and I'll get the bonus. Who'd have thought it of quiet, responsible, respectable Merle?

As Jake drove through the town centre, heading for their house on the east side of Kerikeri, Merle jumped as a siren cut through the air, ringing out loud across the empty streets. "What the hell? Has Germany invaded Poland or something?"

Jake grinned. "It's the town's fire siren. The fire service in the Northland is mainly voluntary, you see, and when the volunteers hear the siren they know to come running."

Merle frowned. "But Neon said he's on nightshift tomorrow?"

"Yeah, well, he's not a volunteer."

"What do you mean?"

Bree glanced at Merle over her shoulder. "He's one of the senior station officers in charge of the fire station here. He was the youngest in the North Island to make that position. And they reckon he'll be chief fire officer before he's thirty."

"Oh." Merle felt a tingle all the way down her body. *Of course* he was special. She looked out of the window at the Christmas decorations in the shops. She should have known he did more than rescue cats from trees.

"There were about twenty-five hundred applicants for twenty-five places on the recruit course," said Jake. "And I'm pretty sure he was near the top of that list."

"You should ask him what his training was like," said Bree. "Intense aerobic tests, press ups, dead lifts, shoulder presses... He scored six on all of those."

"Out of what?"

Bree looked at her, eyebrows raised. Merle sighed.

"He broke a local record for dead lifting," said Jake.

Well, that didn't surprise her. The memory of how easily he'd been able to support her weight wasn't going to fade any time soon.

Bree's eyes were twinkling. "How hot are you for him right now?"

Merle looked out the window. The two of them were laughing, but humour was the last thing on her mind. Her heart was thumping, and she felt an unfamiliar surge of something through her blood that made her inhale sharply and her head spin.

Oh no. She closed her eyes. *No, no, no.* She'd only met him twice. True, she had slept with him repeatedly in that short space of time, but even so, it was hardly a lasting relationship.

She couldn't possibly be in love.

This was terrible. Awful. Surely she was wrong. Love was something that built up over time, wasn't it? It developed over months and years, like stalactites—it wasn't something that appeared overnight like fungus. No, she obviously wasn't in love. She was in lust. Yes. She breathed a little easier. That made sense. And who in their right mind wouldn't fall in lust with Neon Carter?

Ella, his previous girlfriend, sprang into her mind, and she remembered overhearing their conversation on the phone. Ella had felt the same way about him. It obviously happened when you were near him for a short space of time—he was gorgeous, warm, funny and sexy—what wasn't to like? But it didn't mean either of them had been in love with him.

Love was what happened after the first flush of lust had worn off and you found out they hated doing the dishes and never put their socks in the laundry basket, and yet you still wanted to be with them. Love was looking after them when they thought they were dying from a measly cold, and putting up with their snoring, and letting them watch the rugby although there was a show you were missing on the other side.

Wasn't it?

Certainly, in Merle's meagre experience, that "zing" you got when you first met someone did not last into a relationship. Not that she'd particularly had the "zing" before. She pictured both Simon and Phil. She'd never felt anything like the attraction she felt for Neon right now. But that wasn't the point.

What was the point? She'd had too much wine. The point was that the "zing" wasn't love. It was lust, desire, hunger, an itch that had to be scratched. Lust was like a flea and if you didn't squash it quickly enough, it would give you an irritating rash. Well, she'd itched her last itch, and Bree and her three hundred bucks could go hang. Like the carefully tended lawn of a stately home, Neon Carter was now officially out of bounds. She'd built up enough hot memories to warm her through for a lifetime, and they would have to do from now on.

Neon watched Jake's car disappear into the distance, listening to the forlorn wail of the fire siren, and gave a long sigh. He wasn't on shift, but he knew he should call the station, just to make sure he wasn't needed.

What an evening. He started to smile as he thought of how relieved she'd been when he'd asked if she wanted to…well, he hadn't finished the sentence. Clearly it had been on her mind as much as his. He'd watched her watching him all evening, conscious she'd been studying him as he talked to his family, aware she'd sighed every time he moved, shivered every time he laughed. He'd played up to it, but then it had backfired on him, because the more aroused she got, the more turned on he got until he could feel her sexual tension across the room as clear as if she'd flashed a huge neon sign. He grinned at the pun. She wasn't even there and she'd made him laugh.

He turned to go indoors and stopped dead as he saw his parents in the doorway. He wiped the smile from his face and stared at them, wary at the twinkle in his mother's eye.

"Thinking about Merle, were we?" Julia asked.

He glared at her. "No."

"Son, you've not been able to lie to me since the day you stole that bag of sweets from the shop and I made you go and give them back."

He shrugged. "Okay, I was thinking about her. So?"

"So... What are you going to do about her?"

He fixed her with a steely glare. "I am not having this conversation."

"Neon..."

He put his hands on his hips. "Stop planning the wedding, Mother. Merle is here on holiday. I've known her for forty-eight hours. She lives thirteen thousand miles away. You think that's a good basis for a long-term relationship?"

Pierre grinned. "But you do like her."

"Dad, she has legs up to here and a C-cup, of course I like her."

Julia pouted. "You can't fool me, sunshine—there's more to it than that."

"No, Mum, really, there isn't." He gave her a frank look. "Do you want me to explain what I mean by that?"

She rolled her eyes. "Go on then, pretend it's all about sex."

"Sorry to disappoint you, but that's exactly what it's all about." He frowned. "Why pick on Merle? Why not Ella? Or Robyn? I went out with her for six months."

"Five and a half months of which you spent either at work or surfing. I don't think that counts." She studied him. She didn't seem put off by his denial. Reaching up on her tiptoes, she kissed him on the cheek. "You'll understand when you have children of your own one day. Parents know about these things."

He gave a snort. "Bollocks."

"Neon, really."

He gave a deep sigh. "I need a drink. I'm going home." He was driving and he'd had the one beer he allowed himself.

Pierre laughed. "Okay, son. We'll see you tomorrow."

Neon kissed Julia, said goodbye to his aunt and uncle and the rest of his family, then got in his car and drove away.

As he threaded through the town toward his house, he pondered on why his mother insisted there was something different about Merle. True, he had called her "special", but it had been a slip of the tongue. It hadn't meant anything. Had it?

Okay, he could admit to himself now he was alone that he liked her. A lot. She made him laugh. A sense of humour was not a quality he had thought important in a woman—in fact he would have said it was a negative factor if anything, after all, uncontrollable laughter tended to have a detrimental effect on penile blood flow. But he had to admit he'd never had so much fun in bed before. Not that they had actually been in a proper bed either time. He smiled. He'd assumed their enjoyment was due to knowing right from the beginning it was only about sex, but he was beginning to wonder if that was it. She enjoyed sex as much as he did, and her enthusiasm, with the fact that she seemed to find him as attractive as he found her, combined to make sleeping with her a thoroughly enjoyable experience.

But that had to be it. It couldn't become anything else, even if he wanted it to. She lived across the other side of the world, and although her sister had moved here, her mother still lived in England, and she also had her career to think of.

No, there was nothing more to be said about the matter. They'd had great sex and that was it. Stuff the stupid bet he'd made, which had only been done in jest anyway. He wasn't going to think about her again.

This promise to himself haunted him when he was awake at three in the morning, picturing her in his mind as he held her and slid into her, her beautiful eyes wide with desire, focussed entirely on him.

Chapter Eight

Christmas Day and Boxing Day passed without Merle seeing Neon again. She went to Jake's parents for Christmas Day and spent Boxing Day at Bree's house by the pool, and although they had several friends around in the early evening, Neon wasn't one of them. She remembered he was on nights and wondered if he'd been out on any emergencies, then had to steer her thoughts away from the thought of him in uniform, rescuing children from a burning building.

She forced herself to turn her attention to her family, and late in the evening while Jake watched a film in the living room, Merle went into her bedroom and dutifully rang her mother. She did so with a sinking feeling, knowing it wasn't going to be an easy conversation.

Sure enough, Susan was predictably melancholic and depressed at being on her own, though Merle could hear people's voices in the background. "It sounds like there are lots of people there with you," she said cheerfully.

"It's not the same as your own family." Susan sniffed. "I miss my girls so much…"

"It won't be long before I'm back again, Mum."

"But Bree won't be with you." Susan burst into tears.

Merle listened to her crying for half an hour, interspersing patient silence with assurances that everything was going to be all right and she would never leave her mother the same way Bree had abandoned her. She suppressed the resentment and irritation that rose within her when she uttered those promises. *She's sick*, Merle told herself repeatedly as Susan wailed on. *She needs someone to look after her, and I'm the eldest. Bree has her own family now—it's up to me to bear this responsibility.*

But even though she was sure the illness was controlling her mother's outrageous accusations and demands, Merle couldn't stop the odd wave of bitterness sweeping over her. It wasn't her fault she was the eldest. What would have happened if she'd met Mr. Right before Bree? What would her mother have done if Merle had already been married, maybe pregnant, and then Bree had met Jake? There was no way Bree would have stayed in the UK out of guilt.

No, Merle knew she would probably have ended up having to look after a young baby *and* her mother at the same time. Of course many other women in the world had to look after ageing parents. Only usually it happened when the daughter was older, in her forties or fifties, with teenagers looking to leave home, not to a woman in her twenties, still single, still childless. It was all so unfair.

But then Susan started talking about how much she missed Merle's father, and all the guilt came rushing back. Susan hated being single. Sometimes Merle thought her mother was more resentful at being left alone than she was upset at her father dying. Then she felt guilty again. It seemed there was no end to that emotion where your mother was concerned.

At some point Bree came into the room, and Merle was well aware her sister was casting her angry looks as she made her promises, but she took no notice. She didn't bear Bree any resentment for escaping while she could, but she did get cross when Bree judged her for the way she lived her life.

Eventually she passed the phone over to Bree, who sat there and listened to her mother's wails for a whole five minutes before standing up, hands on hips. "I'm sorry, Mum, I'm not going to listen to this," she said, making Merle stare in shock. "I've got better things to do. You know I love you, and I'm sorry you miss me, but I'm enjoying my life here and you should be happy for me rather than berating me all the time. I'll speak to you later." She gave Merle the phone and walked out of the room.

Merle listened to her mother rant for another ten minutes before extricating herself from the conversation. She was sitting on the bed, staring at the phone in her hand, when Bree came back into the room.

Bree faced her, arms crossed, her face thunderous. "Why do you put up with her? She asks you to make all those stupid promises—things a parent should never ask of their children."

"She misses you, and she's not feeling well. She's been having headaches again, and she's still convinced the cancer hasn't gone. She's just vulnerable and fragile, that's all."

"That's not all." Bree shook with anger. "She's manipulative and controlling and unreasonable. How dare she make you promise never to leave her? What about your own life? Doesn't it enter her head you might like to travel or move away from England?"

"Bree, she's no different from any other parent of that age group. They never travelled, and in their eyes, when they reach old age, they should be looked after by their children. It's what happened when they were young and it's very difficult for them to see any other way."

"Bollocks. She knows she's got it easy when you're there to wait on her hand and foot. And she's hardly old, Merle, she's only forty-seven, for Christ's sake. She's young enough to meet another man, if she'd stop feeling sorry for herself and get out and start living again. But she won't because it's too difficult and scary, and she feels safe leaving all the hard decisions and the responsibility to you."

Merle shrugged, turning away to look out the window. It had grown dark outside since she'd come into the bedroom—there seemed to be no twilight in New Zealand—it went from light to dark in what seemed a matter of minutes—and she could hear the kiwis calling their sorrowful cry somewhere in the bush, and the mournful hoot of the morepork. "I'm the oldest daughter, and I do feel a sense of responsibility toward her. I can't abandon her, Bree. She's lonely and sick. I feel sorry for her and guilty when she's on her own."

Bree put her hands on her hips. "Don't give me all that responsibility crap. We don't know she's still sick—they've given her the all clear. All that stuff she says about still feeling the cancer, it's probably all in her head—and I don't mean a brain tumour. She's not eighty years old with a Zimmer frame and false teeth—she's relatively young and perfectly capable of living independently. But you're as bad as her, you stay with her because it's safe—because if you tell yourself she needs you, you don't have to take chances and get out in the world."

"I do take chances!" Merle was appalled. "What about Neon? I hardly call a one-night stand with a guy playing it safe."

"Merle, sleeping with Neon Carter's about the safest thing you could have done."

"What?"

"Having sex with a commitment-phobic guy who lives on the other side of the world? Where's the risk in that? I mean it's not as if there's any chance of a relationship developing, is there?"

Merle turned and put the phone back on the hook. "No."

"So it was fun and I'm glad you've had a great time, but it kind of proves my point. The two serious—and I use that term loosely—relationships you've had have been with men with less personality than a mouldy piece of cheese. Because they were safe—they weren't going to blow your world apart or make you get off your backside and *feel* stuff."

Merle hugged her arms around her body. A tear ran down her cheek.

Immediately Bree came up and put her arms around her. "Oh shit, what am I saying, and on Boxing Day too. I'm sorry, I didn't mean any of it, don't listen to me, I don't know what I'm talking about. I just feel crap because I ran off and left you with her, and I know she's laying the guilt trip on you and it's not fair."

"No," Merle whispered, "you're right, I know you are. I do play it safe, and I know Simon and Phil weren't exactly James Bond. But I can't leave her, Bree. She's our mother, and even if she is being manipulative, it's only born out of loneliness and fear. And she's not well—you've got to remember that. The cancer frightened her and she's terrified it's back, and she's going to get sick and have to cope on her own."

"I know. I'm sorry."

The two girls hugged for a while, and then Merle told her sister she was going to bed. Bree left her, and Merle undressed and slipped beneath the covers, leaving the curtains open so she could stare outside at the darkness. Neon was at the station, working through the night. Had he thought of her at all? Or had he put her out of his mind completely, glad he didn't have to worry about her going supernova like Ella?

It didn't matter either way. She wouldn't be seeing him again. At least she had the memory of the fun they'd had. She could replay it like a favourite DVD when she got back to

England. But she did feel a pang of loss at the thought that she would never see him, never touch him again. Never have him touch her in that way that made her feel so good. Suddenly she wasn't sure it was better to have loved and lost than never to have loved at all.

No, she wasn't going to lie there and say she wished she hadn't met him. Of course she was glad. She'd had great fun, and he'd taught her sex didn't have to be clumsy and awkward and occasionally painful because your partner missed his target. He'd been good for her because he'd made her realise she needed more from a relationship than a warm body. She wanted that "zing", that attraction all the time, and she knew she wouldn't rest until she found it again. And if she didn't find it again, well, she would have to do without.

A sudden wave of panic swept over her. Stay a spinster for the rest of her life and never experience love, or sex, or have babies, ever? That wasn't going to happen, surely. He wasn't the only man out there who was good in bed—there must be others who could make her feel the same way. Weren't there? Of course there were.

She didn't believe in soul mates. There wasn't one man in the world she was meant to be with. And even if there was, he wasn't Neon Carter. There was a man out there who was gorgeous and fun, *and* with whom she had lots in common. The relationship wouldn't be based on sex. Good sex. Passionate, fun, hot, raunchy, blow-your-mind sex. There were more important things you needed in a relationship.

Trouble was, at that moment, lying there imagining Neon's hands on her, Merle couldn't think of a single one.

Monday dawned bright and sunny—again. Merle was

starting to get used to the beautiful weather. At one point she'd asked Bree and Jake how long it was likely to be before the weather broke, and they'd both burst out laughing, explaining though it did rain in the Northland—heavily and frequently— you were guaranteed beautiful sunshine at some point every day during the summer.

In the morning, she took a leisurely walk into the town centre, only ten minutes from their house. She browsed through the shops, buying a few souvenirs to try to convince her mother New Zealand wasn't the worst place in the world, and then she had a coffee and a muffin in one of the cafes, sitting at a table on the pavement, surrounded by palm trees, looking up at the brilliant blue sky.

She returned slowly, enjoying the warmth of the sun on her limbs, arrived at Bree's house around one o'clock and saw a car she didn't recognise out the front. She walked around the back of the house, only realising who the car belonged to when she saw him lying on a lounger on the decking with Jake, stretched out, sunglasses covering his eyes and his hands behind his head.

"Oh crap." She ducked into the house and walked through to the kitchen where Bree was preparing a salad.

"Hey, did you have a good walk?" said Bree.

"Great. Bree—what's he doing here? How come every time I walk into a house he's flat on his back, lying in wait for me?"

"Right back at you, Cameron." Neon's voice carried to them clearly through the open windows.

Merle swore. Bree burst out laughing. "You kind of walked into that one."

Merle glared at her and walked outside to stand over him, hands on hips. "What are you doing here? Aren't you supposed to be in bed?"

He lifted his glasses and looked at her, his warm brown eyes filled with amusement. "Are you offering?"

Jake snorted and Merle shot him a look. "I meant sleeping. Haven't you come off shift?"

"I've had a few hours. I don't usually sleep much the first night as it makes it harder to get back into a routine."

"Oh. So what made you decide to come over and torture me, then?"

He gave her an exasperated glance. "I'm just lying here having a Coke—if anyone's doing the torturing, it's you, standing there with your see-through skirt and no bra, as per normal."

Jake sighed and stood up. "I think I'll go in—I'm getting a headache." He walked off.

Laughing, Neon replaced his glasses and lay back on the lounger. "Sit down for God's sake, you're casting a shadow over me."

Sighing, she sat on the chair beside him. "So why are you here?"

He tilted his head toward her. "I came to see you."

"Oh."

He reached out a hand and picked up hers where it rested on the arm of the chair. "I can't stop thinking about you."

Her lips curled slowly. "Me neither."

He linked his fingers with hers. "Look, do you mind if I speak plainly?"

"Of course not."

"Cards on the table and all that. I know on the beach you were looking for some fun—nothing serious. And Christmas Eve, well, don't quite know what happened there. Hormones took over, I guess. But we're both quite clear on the fact you're

101

only here for another week and then you're flying out. You live in England, I live in New Zealand, and there'll be, like, a gazillion miles of land and sea between us. Right?"

"Right." She looked at their hands.

"After saying that, you're fun and I enjoy your company. And I've got four days off now. So I wondered... Do you want to spend some time together?"

Neon watched his idea settle over her like a soft, silky sheet. She blinked a few times and studied their hands again. He rubbed his thumb along her knuckles, not missing her shiver of response. She was debating whether it was wise for them to spend time together. He knew, because he'd been thinking the same thing for the past two days.

Bar going out with other women, he'd done everything he could to put her out of his mind. He'd had a couple of offers at the party of a friend he went to on Boxing Day, but somehow every time he thought about hooking up with another woman, Merle popped into his head. When he remembered the way she'd practically dragged him into the bathroom at his aunt's house, he knew he didn't want anyone else, not while she was available.

Anyway, there wasn't any risk involved in spending time with her. There was no chance she'd misunderstand and think he was interested in something more than a few days of fun. That was all she'd wanted, anyway, when she kissed him on the beach.

Her eyes were cautious, however, and for a brief moment, he thought she was going to turn him down. Why? Had she met someone else? Perhaps she'd enjoyed the excitement of their encounters so much she'd decided to give one of Jake's friends a try. The thought made his stomach knot, although he had no claim on her.

Then, however, her lips began to curl and he felt a flood of relief.

"Four days?" she asked.

"Four whole days." He studied her, wondering why the thought of another man dragging her off to the bathroom to have sex made him so angry he could punch a hole in the wall. "You haven't made any other…assignations?"

"Assignations?" Her eyes danced. "Well, I did have a soiree yesterday and I'm due to visit the king's court tomorrow…"

He lifted his glasses again and glared at her. "You know what I meant."

She laughed. "No, I haven't had any other dates. Why?" Her eyes gleamed. "Are you jealous, Carter?"

"Of course not."

"Of course not," she echoed. Standing, she leaned over him, hands on the arms of his chair. She obviously wasn't aware her white camisole had gaped away and he had a wonderful view of her breasts. He glanced at them, then looked up and saw her smiling and realised she knew perfectly well he could see down her top. Hmm, who was manipulating whom here?

She looked pointedly at his shorts and he followed her gaze, realising his growing ardour was perfectly visible through the thin fabric. He looked back up at her. "Is this the sort of thing I can expect over the next few days? You teasing me to insanity?"

"Absolutely. Is that a complaint?"

"No." He reached a hand behind her head and pulled her down for a kiss. Her lips were cool, and she opened her mouth and brushed his tongue with hers softly.

He sighed and released her, and she sat back on the chair, smiling. He must be mad. It was going to be torture being around her all the time. He couldn't spend twenty-four hours a day in bed with her. Could he? He shook his head. "Okay, what would you like to do? I'm at your disposal."

"Well, I haven't seen much of the area—Bree and Jake took me to the Stone Store, Te Waimate and Rainbow Falls but that's about it."

"Where do you fancy today?"

She thought about it. "I'd like to see some tropical plants. I like plants."

"Garden centre?" He grinned. "Only kidding. I'll take you to the Puketi Forest. That'll blow your mind if you like trees." Finishing off his Coke, he got to his feet and went inside and asked Bree for some insect repellent. She handed it to him, grinning, and he realised she'd heard every word they'd been saying outside.

"You shouldn't eavesdrop." He took the bottle, glaring at her.

"It's the only way I find out anything around here." She poked her tongue out at him, then winked.

Merle waited for him to come back out, her brain arguing with her heart as to whether spending more time with him was a good idea. Her heart won. It might not be sensible, but who was sensible on holiday? Besides, she wasn't in love with him— she was in lust with him. And that wasn't a problem. She had to remember to make sure she didn't let the one turn into the other.

When he reappeared, he crouched in front of her, a bottle in his hand. He lifted her long skirt to her knee and put her foot in his lap. Spraying his hands a couple of times, he rubbed the liquid along her shins and around her feet. "Don't want you to get bitten." He ran his warm palms down her calves. "Those sandflies are bastards."

"Thanks." Her cheeks grew warm, but he didn't notice, too busy paying attention to her legs. After that, he sprayed his hands again and ran them up her arms and neck, stroking her hands and paying particular attention to her elbows. It was an oddly intimate and strangely non-sexual gesture—until he reached her chest. He ran a finger across her breastbone and dipped it into her cleavage. "Don't want them biting there."

She smacked his hand away and he laughed. "Come on. Let's get going."

"I'll get my bag." She went into the house, picked it up and walked back out. On the way, she passed Bree in the kitchen, who smiled as their eyes met. "Don't say anything." Merle pointed a finger at her sister.

Bree laughed. "Have a great time. And behave!"

"Wouldn't be any fun if we did," said Neon from behind them, bringing in his empty Coke bottle and giving Bree a grin. "Come on, tiger." He grabbed Merle's hand. "We've got exploring to do."

Chapter Nine

Merle slid into the passenger seat of his car, smiling as she glanced around, thinking how much a car could tell you about its driver. Neon's was surprisingly neat inside, with no empty food packets or beer cans like she'd seen in other men's cars, but the floor was covered with a layer of sand.

He got in beside her and started the engine, reversing out of the drive and then heading for the town centre. He smiled at her, and she was conscious of how intimate it was, sitting in a car with a guy. His right leg rested inches from hers, deeply tanned, with dark brown, slightly curling hairs. Obviously he would have to do lots of regular exercise to keep fit for his job. The thought of him working out, getting hot and sweaty, made her heart beat faster.

"Enjoying the view?"

She looked up and grinned. "Jake told me about your training. It sounded pretty intense."

"It was. Fun though."

"You love your job," she said, smiling.

"I do."

"What's it like being senior station officer?"

"You're not on the front line so much, which is a shame in a way because I liked that. But I get to go on some of the more serious calls."

"You're still allowed to play with your hose?"

He laughed out loud. "Whenever I can."

She smiled. "Bree said you were on line to make chief fire officer by the time you're thirty."

"Did she now?"

"How old are you?"

"Forty-two."

"Neon..."

"Twenty-seven, twenty-eight on Thursday."

She stared in surprise. "It's your birthday this week?"

"Yes." He winked at her. "I expect a present."

"I'm sure I can find something to give you."

Laughing again, he reached out and held her hand. "You do make me laugh, you're good for me. Come on, tell me about yourself. I know you lecture in history. What period?"

She settled back in her seat. "I've taught right from prehistoric through to Renaissance but I specialise in Early Medieval, what they sometimes call the Dark Ages."

"King Arthur?"

She grinned. "That sort of period, yes, only usually based more in fact."

"Sutton Hoo? The Venerable Bede? Jorvik?"

She raised her eyebrows. "Yes, very much so."

"Don't look so shocked—my father's a history teacher, remember? I happen to like history."

She smiled and looked away, studying the view, seeing the landscape changing from townhouses to larger houses, surrounded by paddocks with cows and horses. He liked history. She couldn't believe it. Did Fate have it in for her? Why

107

was she being tortured like this?

He took the main state highway north. "Do you live with your mum?"

She kept her gaze on the fields, aware she had tensed. "I do now. I moved back in when Mum fell ill and needed looking after."

"What was wrong with her?"

"Breast cancer. She didn't cope well. I mean who does, I suppose, but she was particularly bad. Dad died two years ago, you see, and it hit her hard. She suffers from depression and she really struggled." Just talking about it was difficult.

"But she's all clear now?"

Merle frowned. "The doctors say she is. But I'm not so sure. She keeps talking about the cancer and how she can feel it inside her. I don't know if it's artistic licence or something more sinister. I keep telling myself it's just fear talking, but...I don't know." She sighed. "I never realised before, how terrible cancer was. I mean of course I know it's a horrific disease, but I didn't realise what effect it had on your character, how it could change you as a person. It's like mistletoe, you know, the way it grows inside trees, and sometimes kills them off. It's insidious, and it's almost like it's possessed her. I'm sure it's still there. When she talks, I can hear it talking through her mouth. It scares the crap out of me."

Neon gave her a sympathetic smile and squeezed her hand. "And she took it bad when Bree left?"

She glanced over at him. He studied her briefly before returning his gaze to the road. Bree must have spoken to him about it, or maybe Jake had told him. "You could say that."

"That must make it difficult for you."

She sighed again, heavily. "It's a long and rather dull

argument. Bree thinks Mum's trying to control me, to make me feel guilty. I know Mum can be manipulative—she used to be a control freak even before she got sick. But I can't accept that's all that's behind her demands. She's really scared. And I can't just abandon her." She studied her fingernails. She'd said too much—she didn't want to talk about this. This wasn't why she'd agreed to go out with him. She wanted fun and escapism—she didn't want to think about why she had to go back and how difficult and constrictive her future would be.

The road turned to metal and the paddocks opened up to fields, wide and spacious, not a hedgerow in sight. No medieval strip farming here. He cleared his throat and started asking her what music and films she liked, and she felt a sweep of relief he'd picked up she didn't want to talk about her mother.

They established they both liked The Beatles, both disliked country and western, and he preferred blues while she preferred jazz. She discovered he loved *Gladiator* and *Robin Hood: Prince of Thieves* (which she adored) and *Kingdom of Heaven* (which she could take or leave), and that he had a secret collection of the *Star Wars* movies, which he admitted to reluctantly but was pleased when she said her favourite was *The Empire Strikes Back*. They found they both adored *House* and *The West Wing*, and spent a pleasant five minutes arguing about their favourite episodes.

"Actually," he said, "I think we should forget about going out and spend four days in bed, watching *The West Wing* and eating ice cream."

She sighed. "That sounds like absolute heaven."

He glanced across at her. "How about we make it a date for my birthday? The whole day in bed, watching *The West Wing*? I can't think of a nicer way to spend it."

She stared at him in surprise. "But you'll want to see your

family and friends, surely."

He shrugged. "I can see them any day of the year. You've got a use-by date."

She smiled, warmth spreading through her at the thought that he wanted to spend his special day with her alone. "Okay. But only if it's chocolate ice cream."

"Chocolate fudge brownie."

"With chocolate sauce."

"And marshmallows."

She rolled her eyes. "Well, that's just plain dirty."

Laughing, he slowed the car as it came up to a T-junction, the forest rearing in front of them in a sheet of green. He turned right, the car wheels scrunching on the gravel, and drove a short distance to the parking area, empty of cars in typical New Zealand style, and parked right in the middle. They got out and he locked the car then took her hand, leading her across to the beginning of the walkway.

"Wow." She admired the beautifully crafted wooden pathway that wound into the forest. "This is amazing."

"I know. The kauri trees are huge. They were used as masts for early ships—Captain Cook refitted with a kauri mast. The early settlers traded the kauri gum abroad. It was used in settings for false teeth." He grinned at her. "I'm full of useless facts."

She laughed. He kept hold of her hand, his fingers warm, as they walked, pointing out the occasional bird to each other, admiring the huge ferns. It was like being in the jungle, such a completely different world. The pathway meandered deep into the forest. Mosquitoes brushed their limbs, although they didn't bite, thanks to the repellent.

Arching palms and huge kauri trees towered over their

heads, fantails flitting between the ferns. The curled fronds reminded her of his tattoo. She brushed it as they walked along the wooden walkway, her fingers tracing the curling black lines, and he looked at her, smiling. A spark jumped between them, quick as a camera flash, sharp as a bee sting, and her heartbeat quickened. She had him all to herself for four days, and she still couldn't keep her hands off him.

She paused and leaned on the wooden rail, pretending to read a plaque, although her concentration was entirely centred on him. He left her side and crossed the walkway to read a display, coming to stand behind her, leaning a hand either side of her on the rail, his chest warm against her back.

Her heart thudded. It was so humid in the forest she could feel a trail of sweat between her breasts and down her back. His arms were a deep brown next to her pale skin, the muscles toned like carved and polished wood, the tattoo curling up like a fern wrapping around him. He oozed health and vitality and strength, making her realise how it must have been in prehistoric times when women looked for a man who could keep them safe, protect them and hunt for them. She could imagine him as a caveman, dragging her through the forest by her hair. Not that he was a Neanderthal—far from it. She knew she had underestimated him on first impression.

He leaned forward, looking at one of the plaques, and his chest and hips pressed against her. Her lips started to curve. "Is all the talk of logging and tree trunks turning you on?"

"I think it's the thought of getting wood, actually." He chuckled, his lips brushing her ear, turning her giggles to sighs as he sucked the lobe into his mouth and nibbled it.

He slid his left arm across her body, pulling her tight against him, his fingers finding her breast, stroking her nipple, while with his right hand he began to raise her long skirt, a handful at a time.

Her eyes widened. "Here? In public?"

"We'll have to avoid all the crowds." He glanced around and she followed his gaze, seeing only black tuis with the white bobble at their throats, and the beautiful turquoise-and-cream of a kingfisher flash in the undergrowth.

She rolled her eyes. "I know there's nobody here now, but what if somebody turns up?"

"Well, you keep watch while I have a quickie."

She started laughing, then caught her breath as his warm hand finally found her thigh, brushing up it and around to cup her bare bottom.

"No underwear again? You are a wicked girl."

"Wicked's my middle name." She sighed as he pressed his hips against her. He was hard as a rock against her butt.

He moved his hand around her hips to her stomach, threading his fingers through her pubic hair, into the hot, wet centre of her. He gave a sexy laugh against her ear. "Oh my. It looks like I'm not the only one turned on today." He slid two fingers deep inside her, making her inhale sharply, then moved them up, coated and slick, to rub against her.

She sighed out loud, leaning back against him as he stroked her, his touch gentle but insistent, his breath hot on her ear as he whispered to her all the things he wanted to do to her, making her blush, his hand growing wet with her arousal.

He groaned and for a brief moment pulled away. She heard the rustle of paper, and then seconds later felt his warmth at her back again, his arms sliding around her, enveloping her.

"You came prepared," she said between gasps of breath.

"Always, when you're around." He pushed her legs apart and she lifted her hips, letting him slide into her in one smooth movement. Then he pulled her back into his arms, his left tight across her, playing with her nipple, his right hand delving back into her moist warmth, even as he started moving inside her.

Merle arched her back, pushing against him. His arms held her tightly, his fingers relentless, and she knew he wasn't going to let her go until she came. The thought was enough to make her orgasm bloom, and she gasped as she felt her thighs and stomach begin to tighten.

"Neon..."

"I know, I can feel it. Come for me, baby." He deepened his thrusts and she cried out as the wave swept over her, her internal muscles tightening in exquisite pulses, and then she felt him shudder and knew his own climax had taken him, and his palm pressed against her warm folds, pulling her against him as he swelled, hot and hard, inside her.

Afterward, he turned her into his arms, holding her tightly as her breathing began to slow. She nuzzled into him and he smiled, stroking her hair back off her forehead, kissing the top of her head. Suddenly he felt guilty for taking her right there, in the middle of the forest. Yes, it was exciting, but she deserved more than a quick shag because he felt horny. He wanted her in a bed where it was comfortable. He wanted her where she could lie back while he pleasured her, and not have to worry somebody was going to come around the corner.

"Come on." He took her hand and led her slowly back up the path. They threaded through the walkway to the car, and he opened the door for her, getting in the other side.

He reversed out and set off back to town. Merle sat quietly, humming to herself, sleepy and relaxed, and he reached out and held her hand, wanting to touch her.

He put some music on the iPod and they drove listening to

113

it for a while, not speaking, although he didn't let go of her hand, and his mind was whirring. When they reached the main road, he put the car in park and turned in his seat.

"Do you want to go home yet?"

She checked the clock on the dashboard—it was nearly three o'clock. She shrugged. "I'm not desperate, but I don't mind if you want to—you must be tired. I haven't forgotten you were on nights yesterday."

"Nah." He smiled. "I only need four or five hours' sleep. Okay, I'm taking you up to Mangonui. There's the best fish and chip shop in New Zealand there, and beautiful views. I'll continue your education on the Northland." Seeing her smile and feeling a wave of happiness, he turned the car left and headed up toward Doubtless Bay.

As they drove, he asked her to tell him more about the subjects she taught at university. He'd sensed earlier she didn't want to talk about her mother or her responsibilities back home, but he did want to know what she was interested in. She told him about the digs she'd trained on, and her favourite historical sites. She seemed thrilled when he revealed he had a secret fascination with armour and weaponry. They spent a pleasant half an hour or so talking about medieval wars and battle tactics, and the benefits of the longbow over the crossbow. It was not a conversation he could recall having had in the past. Nor could he imagine having it with any other woman. That thought made him frown.

Before long, they were pulling into the harbour where he parked right on the waterfront. They walked up to the fish and chip shop and he bought them hoki and chips and squid rings and prawns and a heap of other stuff, and laughed as she tried everything, grease running down her fingers and chin, squealing as he squirted her with lemon.

Afterward, they walked slowly past the shops back to the car, and when they got there, he put his arms around her and kissed her languidly, the sun warm on them, the smell of salt in the air.

He pulled back and looked at her. She sighed happily, smiling at him, reaching up to smooth a lock of his hair he realised must be sticking up. He turned his head and kissed her palm.

"Stay with me tonight," he said before he could change his mind.

She looked up, her blue eyes wide. "Really?"

"Really. I want to make love to you slowly, lying in a soft bed without the risk of stones digging in my back. I must be getting old."

She blinked slowly. "Make love?"

He hadn't used the term before. It was the first time one of them had admitted they were doing more than having sex. His heart rate increased, but he decided to play it light. He didn't want to scare her off. "Well, you know, shag, screw, fuck. It's not like we're engaged or anything."

She laughed. "How could I resist such an invitation? Okay, Mr. Romantic, you've won me over."

He tightened his arms around her. "Good." He kissed her again. Why did he feel such a surge of pleasure at the thought of taking her home?

They got in the car and he drove them back along the state highway, holding her hand all the way. They sang to songs on his iPod. He felt ridiculously happy.

As they got nearer to Kerikeri, Merle frowned. "I'll have to get some things from Bree's."

"What do you need? Don't worry about clothes. You won't

be needing those."

She nudged him. "Don't embarrass me."

He laughed. "How can I possibly embarrass you after what we've done?"

"I don't know. You have a special knack." She sighed. "I wish I could sneak in when she wasn't there. She's going to love this."

"Jake said they were meeting friends at five. They'll probably be out."

"Good. We'll go in and out, black ops."

Shaking his head, laughing, he took the turn-off for Bree's house, and before long they were pulling in the drive. Bree had given Merle a key and she let herself in. Following behind her, Neon heard her rustling in her bedroom, packing a small bag. Then she came out. "I'll leave her a note," she said, finding the back of an envelope and a pen. She wrote, *Staying with Neon. See you later. Stop smiling. BTW you owe me two hundred dollars.*

His smile faded. "Two hundred bucks? What's that for?"

"Oh, I loaned her some money a few days ago." She smiled. "Come on."

He followed her back out to the car, aware she was lying and was referring to the bet Jake had told him about. Was that all what this was about? Winning a bet with Bree?

Suddenly he remembered the bet he'd had with Jake. He hadn't thought about it all day, but the memory of it made him uncomfortable. He couldn't possibly be angry with her for doing the same thing.

She slid in the car beside him with her bag and clipped herself in. He did the same. She glanced across at him, but he didn't say anything as he started the engine.

"Are you okay?"

"Fine." He started to reverse.

"Neon."

He stopped and looked across at her.

She frowned. "What's up? Have you changed your mind?"

He studied her. Her eyes were carefully guarded, the way they were when her mind worked furiously, trying to puzzle him out. She had only been joking around with her sister. What the hell was wrong with him?

He smiled. "Of course not." On impulse he leaned across and kissed her. Her mouth opened under his, her hand coming up to slide through his hair, and he thought of how she'd welcomed his touch in the forest, how she'd blushed when he whispered to her some of the things on his mind. Nothing mattered but these four days, nothing else was important, not Bree or Jake, not their parents, not Ella or anyone else from their past. It was just him and her, enjoying the moment until it was time to move on. Suddenly he was desperate to take her to his house, to get her on her own, on his territory.

"Come on." He drew back. "I'm going to take you home."

Chapter Ten

Neon drove along Bree's road, halfway along taking a left turn into a quieter lane that wound toward the inlet. Merle glanced across at him and he smiled, and she felt a wave of relief. Back at Bree's house, she'd been sure he'd had second thoughts about inviting her back, but it seemed his doubt had passed.

He slowed down and turned in to a long drive that meandered past an orchard filled with mandarin trees and then curled around in front of a long, low house.

"How long have you lived here?"

He parked and turned off the engine. "About six months. I had a flat in town before but it was quite small and...I like space."

She got out, immediately smelling the lemon trees surrounding the property, and followed him up to the front door, carrying her bag. He opened the door and indicated for her to go in before him, and she walked into the house.

It was light and airy, the pale walls and light-coloured furniture adding to the feeling of space. The living room housed a sofa and chairs and a huge TV. The kitchen was brand new, and she could see bedrooms along the hall. The floor was polished wood, and the walls held several large, colourful abstract paintings.

She walked around the living room while he shut the door. She ran her fingers along the bookshelves, seeing books about rugby, surfing and history, especially the First and Second World Wars, and then bent to examine his DVD collection, smiling as she saw the seven seasons of *The West Wing* all lined up at the front.

She continued her perusal, aware he was watching her. An acoustic guitar stood on a stand by one of the armchairs. "You play guitar?"

"No, I like looking at it."

She poked her tongue out at him, walking over to the window. A large area of lawn ran down the hill, disappearing into bush. A few metres up the path, she could see the railings of a swimming pool. "You have a pool?"

"Yes. Not a big one, but hey, size isn't everything." He threw his keys onto a nearby table, smiling.

"It's lovely here, Neon, you must be very proud of it."

He shrugged, but she could see the compliment had pleased him. He pointed along the hall. "The bedroom's through there. It has an en suite if you need the bathroom." He checked his watch. "It's still quite early. You want to go for a swim?"

"Oh, I didn't bring my swimsuit, I didn't think."

He walked over to her, his eyes alight with amusement. "Who needs a swimsuit?" He kissed her.

"Skinny-dipping? I'm shocked."

He laughed and disappeared into the bathroom, then reappeared with a couple of towels. "Come on." He took her hand and led her out the large glass doors and up to the pool. Merle glanced around. There wasn't a house in sight. To the south, bush led to the Waitangi Forest. Far to the north up the hill, a line of tall trees hid them from the sight of anyone else.

119

Any place less like England she couldn't imagine.

She turned back to the pool, which was a decent size and made of dark blue fibreglass that sparkled in the sunlight. There were steps at the shallow end. The crystal-clear water looked hugely inviting.

He was already stripping off, dropping his All Blacks T-shirt onto one of the pool chairs. He slid off his shorts, winking at her, and stood there for a moment with his arms behind his head, turning his face up to the sun and stretching, completely naked.

"Oh my." She pulled off her own top, sighing. How on earth was she going to make it through these four days without jumping on him every five minutes?

He didn't seem to hear her though, and, walking up to the edge of the pool, dived neatly in, surfacing halfway along, swimming to the end in clean, strong strokes. Once there, he turned and rested on the edge, watching her. "Come on, slowcoach."

Sighing, she slid off her skirt, doing the same as him, stretching and enjoying the feel of the sun on her body. She felt decadent and naughty standing there naked, but there was no doubt it was a lovely feeling.

Neon watched the sun glinting off her pale body, wondering why he found her so attractive when she was different from the rest of the women he'd been with. Perhaps that was why. He'd never have thought he'd find such white skin a turn-on. He'd always equated tanned skin with healthiness and usually the thought of the pasty complexions of the cooler climes turned him right off. However, standing there, her arms raised in a sun salutation, Merle looked like a carved statue, her skin white as marble, her beautiful strawberry-blonde hair piled on her head like a Greek goddess.

"Is it cold?" she said, finally dropping her arms.

"Nah. It's like a bath." He knew she wasn't the sporty type and wondered if she would be one of those women who had to get in inch by inch, refusing to get their hair wet. But she stood on the edge, her toes curled over the tiles, took a deep breath and dived in nimbly, surfacing and swimming up to him in neat strokes. "You're a swimmer," he said admiringly as she touched the side.

"It's the one sport I'm any good at." She laughed, lifting herself in the water to sit astride him and kiss him, then pushing off with her legs, leaving him in the backwash.

He caught up with her easily, kissing her leisurely, enjoying the sensuality of the water on their bodies. Then they drifted to the side and looked across at the beautiful view of the forest.

She leaned her head on her arms, droplets of water sparkling on her skin, and studied him, smiling. "No wonder you leave a trail of heartbroken girls behind you, Neon Carter. You're quite a catch."

He smiled. He loved the way she liked to compliment him. "You think?"

"You're a surfer, a rugby player and a firefighter, for heaven's sake. You own your own home, complete with pool. And your body, well... Let's say there's no disappointment in that area." She smiled. "Of course you're a catch. The woman who manages to keep you is a very lucky lady. I hope she realises how lucky she is."

He studied her. Her eyes had turned cool, emotionless, though he now knew that was because she was trying to hide her feelings. "I don't know. I may never get married."

"That would be a waste. Don't you think you'll get back with Ella?"

"No..." He drew out the word vehemently, making her laugh. "God, no."

"Have you ever lived with anyone?"

"I'm guessing you're not including Jake."

"I was referring to the female half of the species, yes."

He brushed a couple of leaves off the tiles. "No."

"Why not?"

He shrugged. "I guess I've never met anyone I've wanted to do that with."

"What's the longest relationship you've had?"

He turned to study her. "Six months. Not a great track record, I know."

"When did you break up?"

"Oh, over a year ago."

"So she never came here?"

He started to smile. "No. I've never brought a woman to this house."

She looked surprised. "Why not?"

He glanced over at the house. "Don't know. It's my place. I've never wanted to share it with anyone before."

He looked back at her. She wasn't smiling now. She was frowning. Had that remark upset her? Was she worrying he was getting all serious on her?

"Of course I'm expecting you to sleep in the garage." He caught her by the waist and brought her legs around him. "I'll stick a mattress there and a bucket in case you need it during the night."

She started laughing and he kissed her. He was curious now. "What about you?"

"What about me?"

"Have you lived with anyone?"

"No."

"What's the longest relationship you've had?"

"Same as you, I guess, about six months, but it wasn't serious." She didn't elaborate.

He kissed her again. "He must have been mad to let you go."

She shrugged. "He didn't seem bothered at the time."

Neon shook his head, puzzled. "But you're, like, the perfect woman. What more did the stupid bastard want?"

She burst out laughing. "Nicely put!"

"I'm just saying..." He frowned. He wouldn't think about some other guy kissing and touching his Merle. That way led to madness.

Hold on, *his* Merle? When had she become *his* Merle? This was only a temporary situation. She was on loan to him—he had to remember that.

She sighed now, running her wet hands up his body. "I've never swum naked. It's a lovely feeling."

"And it looks great. I love the way these things float." He cupped her breasts in his hands. "At least if you ever fall over the side of a boat you won't have to worry about drowning—you've got your own water wings."

"Neon!"

He laughed, wrapping her in his arms. He had all night to play with her and couldn't believe his luck.

They swam for another half an hour and then got out and went indoors. She grimaced at her reflection. "I might have a quick shower and get the chlorine out of my hair."

"Sure. I'll have a half-hour run, if you don't mind."

She raised her eyebrows. "After night shift and a swim? Aren't you knackered?"

He laughed and smacked her butt. "No, not yet. Don't worry—there'll be plenty of energy left for later."

"Where do you run?"

"Oh, I've got a treadmill and a few weights in the spare bedroom. I'll only be half an hour."

"Okay." She kissed him and walked off into the bedroom. He sighed. He had to wear off some of his energy or he'd be pestering her all night.

Merle took a long, lukewarm shower and then pulled on a light white camisole and a floaty pink skirt before coming out, dragging a comb through her tangled locks. She could hear the running machine still going and walked through to the spare bedroom to see how he was doing. She stood in the doorway, watching him for a while. Facing away from her, he had both of the large glass sliding doors open to let in the cool air, and he wore buds in his ears, his iPod attached to his hip. He ran at full speed, a deep V of sweat staining the navy T-shirt he'd put on, his strong thigh muscles bunching and straightening as he pounded the surface.

She glanced around the room, seeing a bench for lifting weights and lots of different dumbbells, realising for the first time how much physical work he had to do to keep in shape for his job.

He'd slowed the machine now, so she turned and went into the kitchen and opened the fridge, extracted a bottle of spring water and poured a glass, filling it with ice. She took it into the spare room and leaned against the doorpost. He lay on his back on the bench doing chest presses, pushing up the bar with what looked like extremely heavy weights, straightening his arms easily.

She sighed, watching the beautiful muscles on his arms moving. How strong and in control he was. She must be crazy, agreeing to spend the night with him. Talk about self-imposed torture. It was becoming harder and harder to leave him, but she couldn't bear to be apart from him. And somehow, she guessed he felt the same way. His comment about never having brought a woman to his house had made her tingle all over. He hadn't wanted to share it with anyone before, he'd said. Why had he brought her here, then? Was he saying he felt differently about her than he'd felt with the other women he'd dated?

He lifted the weights one last time, locking the bar onto the rests, and sat up, running a hand through his hair, surprised to see her there. He got to his feet and came over to her, smiling. "Sorry, have you been waiting long?"

"Not at all. I was...admiring the view." She glanced out of the window, but when she looked back, he grinned and she knew he understood what she really meant.

She handed him the glass, and he thanked her and drank it in one go, wiping the back of his hand across his mouth, watching her. She was barefoot, and he seemed so much bigger than her, tall and broad, his tanned skin glowing with sweat, the picture of a healthy, lusty male. She looked up at him, her heart starting to pound as the mischievous look appeared in his eyes. "What?" she said as he smiled.

"Your eyes are like saucers again. That's how you looked the first time I met you on the beach, and look what happened there."

"I can't help it—you look good enough to eat."

"Well, let me have a shower and I'll see what I can do."

"Nuh-uh." She shook her head, stepping closer to him. She caught the bottom of his T-shirt in both hands, lifting it over his head and dropping it to the floor, revealing his wide chest, glistening with sweat. He was smiling wryly now. She put a hand on his chest and pushed him backward until he met the wall with a bump, then stepped even closer. She put a finger under his chin and lifted it, pushing his head up. He did so, looking puzzled, understanding only when she leaned forward and ran her tongue up his chest to the hollow at the base of his throat, pressing her lips there, tasting him.

"Pheromones, huh?" He slid his arms around her, laughing.

She felt dizzy with desire. "Absolutely. That's the second time today I've felt practically prehistoric." She took his hand and walked out of the room, bringing him with her into his bedroom. It was a lovely large room with a king-size bed, beautiful paintings on the wall and a gorgeous view across the bush. The warm, humid air closed around them, and when he switched the fan on above the bed, the cool breeze was delicious on her skin.

She turned, putting her arms around him. "Are you too tired?"

"Never, with you." He ran his hands down her sides, pressing her to him.

"What would you like to do?" She tipped back her head, shaking her hair, looking up at him boldly. "I'm all yours, Neon. If you still want to play with me."

His warm brown eyes turned hot. "All mine?"

"Do with me as you will. Anything you want."

"Anything?" He brushed her lips with his.

"Anything." Her heart hammered. She trusted him and wanted to give herself to him completely. She knew he'd never hurt her or embarrass her, intentionally anyway. How could she feel this way about him when she'd only known him for such a short time?

126

He smiled. "I know exactly what I want to do with you." He lifted off her top and removed her skirt, leaving her naked. Getting rid of his shorts, he moved backward to the bed and climbed on. He threw the pillows onto the floor and lay down, making himself comfortable.

He looked up at her and beckoned her over. The mischievous look was back.

She climbed onto the bed and moved toward him. He beckoned her closer. She moved up to his waist, her heart pounding at the intense look in his eyes. He beckoned again. "Closer. Right up here." He tapped his mouth.

Merle stared at him. Suddenly she realised what he wanted. Her cheeks heated, and she turned, scooting toward the edge of the bed, shaking her head. Oh my, what had she thought about him not embarrassing her?

Laughing, he grabbed her wrist. "Where are you going?"

"I can't..." She refused to look at him. "Neon, let me go."

"No." He pulled her onto the bed and leaned over her, forcing her to look up at him. "What's the matter?"

She met his gaze, speechless, and he lifted up off her, leaning back against the headboard, shocked. "You're kidding me?"

She pushed herself up. "Neon..."

"You're twenty-five and a man's never gone down on you?"

She almost laughed, he looked so horrified. "They never offered, and I didn't like to ask..."

"They never offered?" He glared at her. "What the hell? What sort of jerks have you been dating?"

She did laugh then. He fixed her with a determined gaze. "That settles it." He lay down again. "I'm not leaving this room until that—" he pointed down, "—is on here." He pointed to his mouth.

The very thought made her grow damp with desire, but still she couldn't move. "Neon, I..."

His gaze softened, and he held up a hand. "Come here." She moved forward into his arms, and he held her tightly against him, her head on his shoulder. He kissed her hair, then rolled so he could look at her. "You did promise me anything I wanted."

"I know. I was thinking more...you know...something that turned *you* on."

He laughed. "This *would* turn me on, believe me." He pressed light kisses on her lips, her cheeks, her eyelids. "I want to do this for you. It's a nice thing, from what I can gather. I think you'll enjoy it."

She started to laugh. "I'm sure I will..."

"Come on, tiger, make my day. If you don't, you'll always wonder what it would have been like...with me, at any rate."

He'd implied a man in the future might offer it to her, she realised. She remembered her promise to herself that if she didn't find anyone as nice as Neon, she would remain single. She might never get this offered to her again.

That thought was enough to make her scramble to her knees.

"Okay, you talked me into it."

Grinning, he lay back, getting comfortable, then beckoned her forward. "You might need to hang on to the headboard."

She blushed but moved up to his head and straddled him, feeling him run his hands up her thighs to guide her down. Leaning on the headboard, she closed her eyes.

Chapter Eleven

When his tongue first touched her, she gasped. It was warm and soft, and he stroked gently through the soft folds of her skin, bringing his hand around so he could part her lips with his fingers, accessing the hot core of her.

She leaned her head on her arms as he continued pleasuring her with his mouth, her head spinning, unable to believe what he had offered to do for her. She gave herself over to the sensations as he licked and sucked, his tongue and fingers gentle but firm. She sighed, caught her breath, then sighed again as he experimented with different strokes and pressures, finding out what she liked. Dear God, this should be one of the ten wonders of the world. How had she got to twenty-five without experiencing this?

She knew she wasn't going to last long. The sensations he was causing were too intense for her to bear. His hands slid up her body to cup her breasts, and as he began to roll her nipples gently between his fingers, the pressure began in her stomach, her breathing coming in short gasps.

At that moment, however, he dropped his hands and his mouth lifted from her. The sensations petered out into small ripples, making her sigh with disappointment. Why had he stopped? Did he not want her to come?

After a few seconds, however, his warm tongue brushed her

again, and she gasped. He licked and sucked her until once again she felt the wave begin to build.

For the second time he lifted his mouth from her, and she realised he was teasing her, bringing her to the edge and leaving her to teeter there, the orgasm she desperately wanted out of reach.

When he did it a third time, she nearly burst into tears. "Neon, please…" she begged, resting her forehead on her arms.

His hand stroked her thigh warmly as if to say sorry, then his strong arm came up to rest on the tops of her thighs while his other hand stroked her, his fingers sliding into her as he brushed her with his tongue once again. She came almost immediately, and this time he didn't stop.

As her climax swept over her like a tidal wave, she instinctively tried to rise, but he'd clamped his arm across her like an iron bar, holding her tight to him, and she cried out as her muscles pulsed strongly, his fingers deep within her, his mouth hot, sucking her to ecstasy. It was like no other orgasm she'd ever had, so intense, so breathtaking that for a minute she forgot to breathe out, inhaling until she thought her lungs would pop.

When he finally released her, she lifted herself off him and lay back on the bed, covering her eyes with her arms as her breathing gradually returned to normal. "Oh my God," she whispered, unable to formulate any other thought in her brain.

He shifted on the bed and leaned over her, laughing as she refused to look up at him. "What's up?"

"Nothing."

"Was it not nice?" His voice was teasing, and he pulled her arm away, forcing her to look at him. His eyes were very warm and surprisingly tender.

"Thank you." She blushed.

"You are very, very welcome." He kissed her, and she could smell her arousal on him, taste it on his lips. "But I haven't finished with you yet."

He rolled onto his back, pulling her with him, making her squeal, and she pushed herself up, sitting astride him. "I want to be inside you," he said huskily. "You're so wet and swollen—it's going to be heaven."

She pushed her hips back, feeling him pressing against the now very sensitive part of her.

"Merle, wait."

Oops. She'd forgotten about the condom. She hesitated. "I'm on the Pill, if you want to leave it. I have been since I was eighteen because I used to have heavy periods. But I've never had sex without a condom before so I'm, you know, clean."

"Neither have I."

"It's up to you." She desperately wanted him inside her, but she waited, leaning over him, knowing he had to agree.

She couldn't tell what he was thinking. His brown eyes looked very light, like polished pine. Was he worried she was trying to trick him into getting pregnant? There were women who would do that, she knew. She didn't want him to think that of her. "It's okay." She smiled. "I've got one in my bag, hold on."

Neon's heart raced. Merle went to move off him, but he caught her arm. "No, leave it."

She met his gaze, her eyes like a warm summer sky. Something passed between them—an understanding, a connection. She waited for a moment, as if making sure he didn't want to change his mind. Then she leaned forward and kissed him. As she did so, she pushed her hips so he slid into her warm, velvety softness. She was so wet, so swollen, and he was so sensitive without a condom, he gave a long, drawn-out sigh.

Smiling like a satisfied cat, pushing herself upright, she spread her thighs and arched her spine, dropping her head back so her long hair brushed his legs. He sank so deep into her, and she was so gorgeous, so hot, he nearly came then and there. At that moment, looking at her beautiful pale body, something blossomed inside him, born from a seed planted when he'd told her in the pool she was the first woman he'd invited back to the house. Or had it begun earlier than that, at his aunt's house, when they'd had sex for the second time and suddenly it hadn't been a one-night stand? Or perhaps it had begun on the beach when he'd first seen her standing there, dress blowing in the breeze, completely see-through, causing him to fall off the surfboard?

Whatever the reason, as she lifted her head, her eyes glazed with passion, he knew he was in trouble.

But he wouldn't think about that now. He caught her hand, sliding it down her body and between her legs. "Make yourself come for me."

She stared at him, and his heart sped up. He loved shocking her like this. It was becoming very clear to him that although she wasn't a virgin, she clearly hadn't had any sexual experience worth speaking of, and there was something delicious about suggesting things to her. And the most wonderful thing was that she seemed to be loving every minute of it, as if she had only known there was vanilla ice cream, which was okay, but then he'd taken her into a shop full of shelves of flavours and there were a hundred different varieties open to her, and he was slowly letting her taste them, one at a time.

Except, of course, he only had time for the one shelf. He

wouldn't be the one to introduce her to half the things he wanted to show her. He realised he could spend a lifetime making love to her and never do everything he wanted, with her and to her.

Merle studied him, realisation settling behind her eyes like silt in a river. She was coming to terms with the fact that her arousal turned him on, that if she was having a good time, he was almost certainly going to follow. Jeez, what sort of idiots had she been dating? What guy *didn't* want to go down on his girlfriend, for crying out loud?

Her eyes meeting his, a small smile appeared on her lips. Her fingers started to move, dipping to where he slid in and out of her, to collect some of the wetness, then coming back up to start arousing herself. He put his hands behind his head, smiling, enjoying the view, and she closed her eyes, tipping her head back again, giving herself over to the sensation of her fingers. As he watched, she raised her left hand to her breast, starting to stroke her nipple, and he looked up at the ceiling for a moment, struggling to keep calm, his self-control straining like a wild horse against a rope. He wasn't going to last long at this rate, the sensation of being inside her without any barriers driving him right to the edge.

Luckily, she was already so aroused it only took minutes for her orgasm to build. Her breathing grew more ragged, and her fingers increased their pace as she moved up and down on him, sliding effortlessly, she was so wet.

She opened her eyes. They were half-lidded with desire. "You want me to come for you, baby?"

"Yes," he said huskily, his hands dropping to her hips.

"You want to watch me?"

"Oh yes..."

She widened her thighs again, taking him deep inside her,

and then all her muscles tightened around him as she cried out, tipping back her head, arching her back.

He couldn't hold back any longer and erupted into her, volcano-like, hot and wet, his fingers digging into her hips, his body pulsing until eventually he was spent. He could only lie there, breathing heavily, his energy finally exhausted. She lifted herself off him and came to kiss him, laughing when he couldn't do anything but sigh.

After a while they managed to rouse themselves enough to go and get a couple of tubs of ice cream from the freezer, and they came back to bed and watched *The Empire Strikes Back*, feeding each other macadamia nut and strawberry cheesecake flavours as they quoted the film almost word for word.

Then she made him go and get his guitar and play for her, and he ran through his repertoire of Beatles songs, which she sang to. Afterward, he played a few lazy blues tunes until her eyes started to close. It had grown dark outside, and the kiwis were calling in the bush, the cicadas beginning to play their summer song.

He turned off the bedside light and she curled up beside him, her head on his shoulder. He lay looking at the painting on the opposite wall as she dozed off, his eyes growing heavy with sleep. His body was finally tired, but he wanted to hold on to the moment, thinking how the swirls in the painting were a bit like him and Merle, caught up in one another, entangled until he wasn't sure which legs under the bedclothes were his and which were hers, like ribbons wrapped around a maypole. And not just their legs. Their emotions were entangling too, their feelings entwining, knitting together. It wasn't going to be easy to unravel them when it was time for her to go.

It had been an incredible day. But he shouldn't have

suggested she come back to the house with him. How empty was it going to feel when she finally had to go home?

In the morning, Merle was awoken by somebody pressing small, soft kisses across her mouth and cheeks, and she opened her eyes sleepily, smiling as she saw Neon awake, lying beside her, head propped on a hand.

"Hi." She stretched lazily.

"*Morena.* That's Māori for good morning." He kissed her again. "Did you sleep well?"

"Yes, thank you." She had stirred several times in the night, hot and sticky under the covers, smiling to see him sprawled on his back across the bed, completely free of the duvet, sound asleep. Each time she'd curled up next to him, not touching him, content to watch him breathe until she dozed off again. There was something special about watching a person sleep. Sleeping left you vulnerable, defenceless—you had to trust someone completely to fall asleep with them. The thought warmed her. He had felt comfortable enough to do that with her. He wanted her by his side.

Now she smiled as he caught her hand in his and linked their fingers, then bent his head to kiss her again, languid and leisurely, his tongue brushing hers softly.

"What time is it?" she said when he finally lifted his head.

"Seven o'clock." He traced his tongue across her lips, making her shiver. "No need to get up yet." He placed more kisses along her cheek and toward her ear. "You look lovely like this, all sleepy and blurred."

"I'm not going to be sleepy for very long if you carry on like that." Her heart started to speed up as he traced a hand across her skin, down her belly.

He pulled back and studied her, sweeping light fingers up her arm, across her breastbone, between her breasts. "You can doze off if you want. I won't bother you."

"You call that not bothering me?"

"Hey, I'm just lying here."

She started to laugh as his fingers brushed the flat of her stomach, making it quiver. "That tickles!"

He did it again, grinning, then started to follow his fingers with kisses, ducking under the covers, pulling them over his head. Merle sighed blissfully, giving herself over to the sensations he was producing, closing her eyes as the bright December sunlight filled the room, and outside the tuis called, welcoming in the new day.

Later, she cooked breakfast for him, amazed at how many eggs and slices of bacon he could tuck away, and then he announced he was taking her to Waitangi.

"It's where New Zealand was born," he told her as they drove along State Highway Ten toward Paihia. "Where the Treaty was signed. I'm guessing you know all about the Treaty."

"Some. I know it forms the backbone of your constitution here."

He nodded and told her about William Hobson and James Busby and the missionary Henry Williams, who'd lived at Paihia. He explained the problems with the translation of the Treaty from English to Māori, and how that still affected New Zealanders today. Merle listened, nodding. His passion for his country made her smile but also made her sad.

That morning, while he'd kissed her, she'd entertained a fantasy where he'd told her he would go with her to England, but as he spoke now, she realised even if he wasn't commitment-phobic, which she knew he was, there was no way he'd ever want to leave New Zealand. His whole life was here— the country was ingrained in him as clearly as his tattoo. England was breathtakingly beautiful in places, and had a history that far outshone the youthful "Godzone". But she knew it would never fulfil his love of the sun and wide, open landscapes in the same way.

She pushed the thought to the back of her mind for the rest of the morning, as they spent a pleasant couple of hours in the Treaty Grounds. He took her around the displays, explaining the history of the Treaty, then to the *marae*, or meeting house. She had to take her shoes off and leave them outside as she went in to admire the wooden carvings inlaid with paua shell while he explained some of the Māori beliefs.

"Normally you have to be welcomed onto a *marae*." He held her hand as he showed her some of the carvings. "But this is a public one, which isn't quite the same. At the high school I went to in Kerikeri, all the new students have to go to a *powhiri*—" he pronounced it "porfiri", hardening the *R*, "—where they're welcomed into the Māori 'family'."

"I'd like to see a Māori dance," she said, knowing there was a performance at the main centre in the grounds.

He waved his hand dismissively. "I'm playing rugby tomorrow. We don't normally play in summer but it's a special charity match. If you want to come and watch, we always do the *Ka Mate haka* at the beginning. You won't have to pay for that."

She raised her eyebrows. "Like the All Blacks?"

"Yup." He grinned. "You want me right now, don't you?"

"Absolutely. Quick, get your clothes off."

He laughed, leading her out of the *marae* into the sunshine. "Easy, tiger. We'll be back soon enough."

After they'd finished at the Treaty Grounds, he drove them into the seaside town of Paihia and they had a walk around the shops, then afterward they went over on the foot ferry to Russell. It was a small, beautiful town, and she laughed when he told her in the nineteenth century it used to be called Kororareka, which means "sweet penguin".

There they had lunch, sitting outside in the hot sun, Merle with her floppy hat, trying to protect her delicate English skin. "It's so beautiful here," she told him, looking across the bay. "I can see why they call it Godzone."

"Would you like to live here?"

Merle studied him. Had he meant it as a general topic of conversation? Or was he asking her something else? His eyes were light, not serious, however, and she assumed it had been the former. She gave him a smile as she sipped her ice-cold lager. "It's a beautiful place. I'd love to live here. But I have other obligations. My job. And my mum. I could never leave her. She needs me."

The words stuck in her throat. It was so unfair. She felt a sweep of resentment toward her mother. Even though she'd been unwell, Susan didn't have to make Merle feel so bad about finding a life for herself. She deserved a family and children as much as the next woman, didn't she? Guilt quickly followed the resentment, however, and Merle sighed. She knew she shouldn't blame her mum. Susan was lonely and scared. Of course she wanted her daughters around her. It was hardly an unfair demand.

"I know," said Neon.

Their eyes met for a moment. Was there a flicker of sadness in his, or had she imagined it?

Afterward they came back on the ferry, and she was thrilled when she saw dolphins leaping in front of the boat, as if performing just for her.

He drove them back home and they had a swim, made love, had a shower and made love again. Merle lay on the bed afterward, breathless and exhausted, shaking her head as he got up and said he was going for a workout, amazed at his energy. They ate a light tea and later he brought her back to bed, kissing her slightly sunburned skin, continuing to pleasure her well into the night, as if trying to tell her again and again with his body that, although he couldn't say it, he loved being with her and wanted the day to last forever.

On Wednesday morning, he drove her across country to the Hokianga on the west coast. They walked along the headland and she took photographs of him with the Tasman Sea crashing onto the rocks and the sand dunes in the background, then they had lunch in the picturesque village of Rawene before driving back for his rugby game in the afternoon.

"You can stay here if you want," he told her as he dressed in his rugby shirt and shorts and laced up his boots. "But Bree will probably be going as Jake's playing too."

"There's absolutely no way you'll get me to stay here. A chance to see you playing rugby and doing the *haka*? Are you kidding me?"

He laughed, giving her a hug before ferreting around in a drawer for his mouth guard.

"Who are you playing anyway?"

"I used to play for a local team and they're raising money for charity. It's only a friendly."

That's not what she would have called it, she thought an hour later, wincing as Neon barrelled into an opposing player, crashing them both to the ground.

"Oh my God, they're going to be covered in bruises," she said to Bree, who was jumping up and down beside her.

Bree laughed. "They always are, but it doesn't stop them." She studied her sister, smiling. "Did you enjoy the *haka*?"

Merle looked at her and they both started laughing. Was there a woman in the world who could resist fifteen hulking men performing the *haka*? Right from the start she'd tingled all over as soon as the players began forming in three lines, facing the opposing team, who'd performed a *haka* themselves. She'd watched the All Blacks enough times to know one player acted as the leader, calling out instructions to the others before they all joined in with the main chant. She went breathless as she saw Neon walk between the lines of men, yelling out in Māori for the others to take their warlike stance. Of *course* it would be him, she thought dizzily—who could be more of a leader than this six-foot-four hunk of walking masculinity? He widened his eyes, calling to the others to follow his lead, and her mouth went dry as they all began pounding their chests, performing the *Ka Mate* with a dazzling display of testosterone. If she'd thought she couldn't be more attracted to him, she'd been very wrong. Yet again, the prehistoric, animal attraction, the lust of a female for a strong, powerful male swept over her. And she still had him to herself for the rest of the day and tomorrow. She was already planning what she was going to do to him when they got back to his place.

The match itself was more painful to watch, and she had to turn away several times as tackle followed crunching tackle, although she felt a surge of pride when Neon scored the third try. He slid across the grass and rolled over onto his back exultantly as the rest of his team piled on top of him.

Bree smiled, watching her as she yelled encouragement to

him.

"What?"

"Nothing." She reached up and kissed Merle on the cheek. "I'm glad you're having a good time."

"I haven't been to a rugby match in years."

"I wasn't talking about the rugby."

Chapter Twelve

Merle looked across at her wryly. "I know what you meant."

Bree squeezed her hand. "Jake and I were wondering if you two wanted to come out to dinner tonight."

"Dinner?"

"To the Italian, maybe. We thought it would be fun. I know Neon wants to spend his birthday with you tomorrow—we thought we could have a drink tonight to celebrate."

"That would be lovely." Merle smiled, hoping Neon would agree. Would it be too much like a date? She didn't want to spoil the lovely time they were having by making assumptions, acting as if they were a couple when, in the traditional definition of the word, they were anything but.

When he came over after the match, however, it was clear Jake had already arranged to have a taxi pick them up at six o'clock, and Neon seemed quite happy with it.

They walked back to his car, waving goodbye to Jake and Bree, and she climbed in beside him, raising an eyebrow at the grass stains and grazes on his body.

"Usually it would just be mud," he grunted, starting the engine, "but it hasn't rained for a while."

"Are you sore?"

"Nah. I'm a real man." He flexed his arm muscles before

winking at her and driving off. He had never looked more gorgeous, with his hair sticking up at all angles where it had been grabbed by hands that tried to yank it out of his skull, a large graze on his cheekbone, the collar of his rugby shirt half ripped off and his clothes covered in earth and grass. He glanced over at her, then did it again, starting to smile. "Uh-oh."

"What?"

"Your eyes are like dinner plates again. Am I in trouble?"

"Serious, serious trouble. You'll be lucky to make it out alive."

He grinned, his eyes crinkling at the corners, and she sighed, fidgeting until they got home. When he finally pulled up, she jumped out of the car and, taking his hand, led him forward. She waited impatiently while he insisted on leaving his boots by the door, then took him straight through to the bedroom. Walking up to the bed, she fell backward, pulling him on top of her. He burst out laughing, propping himself up on his elbows. "I'll squash you!"

"I want to be squashed." He was right, he was so heavy he was pressing her into the bed, and she hardly had any air left in her lungs, but the sheer weight of him, the breadth of his chest, the strength in his muscles, was making her crazy.

She raised her arms above her head, stretching out beneath him, pushing up her hips. "Come on, Mr. Rugby-Player-Surfer-Firefighter, take me like a caveman."

His eyes went from zero to a hundred degrees in seconds. "You want it rough, baby?"

"Rough as, Mr. Kiwi."

He laughed, catching her wrists with his hands. He planted hot kisses on her neck, pinned both her hands with one of his own and pulled up her T-shirt to access her nipples, which he licked hungrily, making her catch her breath and sigh.

143

Suddenly he fastened his mouth onto the swell of her breast and sucked, making her squeal. "You'll give me a hickey!"

"You betcha." He ignored her protesting wriggle and continued to take bites out of her, nipping at her ear, grazing his teeth across her shoulder. She swore out loud, and in answer, he pushed up her skirt and pulled down his shorts.

She squirmed beneath him, realising she couldn't get out of his grip—his hand was like a vise. He was going to take her immediately, without a full minute of foreplay, in his rugby clothes, grass-stained and covered in dirt and sweat. She nearly came at the thought.

He stroked her briefly, checking that she was wet, laughing when he found she was. Immediately he slid into her, making her swear again. He closed his eyes momentarily. When they opened, they were hot as the sun.

"Don't close your eyes again," she demanded.

"Yes, ma'am." He pushed hard into her, making her gasp.

She wanted to run her fingers up inside his shirt and feel the warmth and heat of his skin. "Let me go. I want to touch you."

"Nuh-uh." He took a wrist in his other hand, pushing himself up, forcing her to bring her legs up.

"Neon..."

"I'm not letting go. Deal with it."

She tried to pull her hands away but should have realised she wasn't strong enough to do that. She could only lie there as he thrust into her, hard and fast, fixing her there with his gaze as much as with his hands. She looked up at him, thinking she'd fallen so far in love with him she was never going to be able to claw her way back. And when she came, he watched her possessively as if he wanted to drink in her pleasure, his body tightening as he followed her, his eyes watching her the whole way.

Neon released her wrists, guilt sweeping through him as he saw the red marks on her skin. He lifted himself off, lying beside her on the bed. He looked at himself, ashamed. He must smell awful. How on earth did he turn her on like this?

He looked at Merle. She hadn't moved, her arms still above her head, her eyes closed, her breathing gradually calming. He moved closer to her, pressing soft kisses on her face. "Are you okay?"

She opened her eyes and looked up at him, then started laughing. "Oh my God."

He grinned. "Sorry."

"I swear you are trying to make sure I never walk again."

He shrugged. At least that would mean she wouldn't be able to leave him. But he wished he hadn't been quite so rough. Sometimes he forgot his strength. He looked at her breast. She followed his gaze and squealed.

He pulled an *eek* face as he saw the large love bite. "Oh dear."

She gave him an exasperated look, pulling down her T-shirt. "Well, I guess I won't be wearing a low-cut top tonight."

"For that I am sincerely sorry."

She pushed herself up, groaning. "I'm so stiff. I haven't done any yoga for days."

"You do yoga?"

"Are you going to say something about it being a wussy sport?"

He laughed. "Not at all. I used to do it when I played rugby. It's great for flexibility."

"I think I might have to do some now. I need to get my hips back in working order."

"I'm sorry." He kissed her again as an apology.

She smiled. "It's okay. I enjoyed myself, in case you didn't notice." She got to her feet. "How long have we got?"

He checked his watch. "Forty-five minutes. I think I should take a shower."

"Hmm. I'm going to work out on the decking." Arching her back, she grabbed a towel from the bathroom and went outside.

He sighed, went into the shower and ran it hot. He stripped and stood underneath the burning water, scrubbing himself clean. Then, turning it to cool, he let it run over his face. He hoped he hadn't hurt her. That was the last thing he wanted to do.

He thought about their dinner reservation with Bree and Jake. When Jake had asked if he wanted to go to dinner with them, he'd responded without hesitation, thinking it would be fun, the four of them, considering they all got on so well. It was only now that he realised how unusual that was for him. Although they all socialised in a group, if he took a girl out, it was usually alone and most often ended back at her place, certainly since he had moved to the house. It was as if he wanted to keep his love life separate from the rest of his life, and though he hadn't thought about it, he now realised he'd been spending more time alone since being in his house. He wasn't sure why. All he knew was he didn't feel the same way about Merle. When they'd walked across the rugby field after the match, he'd put his arm around her shoulders, wanting everyone to see the beautiful blonde was with him. And now, he wanted to go out tonight with her because he wanted people to see them together, to see how happy they were.

He leaned forward, putting his forehead on the glass. What

the hell was he doing? Tomorrow was their last day together, then he was back at work and very shortly afterward she was flying back to England. He doubted he'd ever see her again, or if she did come back, it would probably be in a few years' time, when she was married, maybe even with kids.

The thought of her with another man made his blood boil, searing through his veins. Would she tell her new man, her husband, that she wanted it "rough as"? Would she drag him into the bathroom and tear his clothes off, unable to wait? Would she demand he open his eyes so she knew he was thinking only of her when he came?

Neon's hand tightened into a fist on the glass. This was crazy. She was just another girl, one of many, not the first, and she wouldn't be the last. She was nothing special.

But as he formed the thought, he knew he was kidding himself. She *was* special, he didn't know why, but he felt differently toward her than he had with any other woman he'd been with. And he only had about thirty-six hours left with her. What was he doing wasting it in the shower?

He turned off the water and towelled himself roughly, then went into the bedroom. He could see her outside, on the deck, arms raised in a sun salutation, and he sighed, pulling on a pair of boxers and his jeans before leaning against the frame of the large doors, watching her. She bent forward gracefully, stretching her back, then widened her stance and stretched to the side with one leg bent in the Warrior Asana, holding the pose for thirty seconds before straightening the leg and bending over to the side in the Triangle pose. She did the same on the other side, and he thought how graceful she was, how elegant. He hadn't noticed before, but she was supple and willowy, her movements fluid and smooth.

When she finished, she stood up with a sigh, doing the sun

salutation once more before turning, her eyebrows rising and her cheeks flushing as she realised he was watching her. "How long have you been there?"

"Long enough." He smiled, opening his arms as she walked up to him. He gave her a hug, wrapping his arms around her, nuzzling her hair. "Did you use to do ballet?"

"Till I was eighteen, yes. Why?"

"I can tell. You're so elegant, like a swan." He kissed her. Then he kissed her again, longer this time.

She pushed him away, laughing. "I've got to get dressed. We're leaving in a minute."

"Spoilsport." He let her go into the room and rummaged through his wardrobe as she dressed. Eventually he settled on a light blue short-sleeved shirt and slid it on, doing up the buttons, listening to her humming one of The Beatles' songs he'd played to her that morning, which made him smile. Then he turned around.

He stared. She stopped in the middle of putting in an earring. "What?"

For the first time since he'd met her, she wore trousers. They were cream and very, very tight around her ass, falling to a slight flare at the bottom, touching the ground over her shoes, which were wedges and several inches high. She wore a tight black top with a deep *V* that only just covered the hickey he'd given her. Although he'd looked at her body often enough over the last few days, it was the first time he realised how shapely she was, and what incredibly long legs she had.

"Wow."

She finished putting the silver hoop through her ear and looked down at herself. "What?"

"Your legs are, like, six miles long."

She laughed. "I don't often get the chance to wear heels, but I think I can get away with it, with your height."

He came up to her, pulling her against him. "You look like a model. You're amazing."

She flushed, clearly pleased with the compliment, though she murmured, "Oh rubbish, hardly." She pushed him away. "I have to do my hair." He leaned against the doorjamb and watched as she scooped the long blonde locks in one hand and twisted them up, securing them with a clip at the back. Blonde strands fell in curls around her long, slender neck.

He sighed as she put a slick of lip gloss on her lips. "Well, you know that's a waste of time."

She shot him an amused look in the mirror as she pressed her lips together. Then she blew him a kiss.

"Oh crap, this is going to be like torture." He walked out of the room in a huff. Why had he agreed to spend the evening with other people? He should have kept her to himself!

As the evening wore on, though, Neon began to realise he was enjoying himself and finally conceded it had been a good idea to go along. The Italian restaurant was intimate and the food was great. The company was fun too. He'd grown up with Jake, and they were more like brothers than cousins. He'd taken an instant liking to Bree, who was sharp, sassy and funny. Together the two girls were witty, teasing and a great double act, teaming up against the boys occasionally, knowing perfectly well how to wind them both up.

Like when Merle cast Jake a glance halfway through the evening and said, "Jake, sweetheart, you do realise that's my leg you're rubbing your foot up," causing great merriment and making Jake stutter with embarrassment.

149

Bree grinned. "Could have been worse, could have been Neon's."

"Do that to me and you'll be swallowing your teeth," Neon told him wryly, making them all laugh.

They toasted him happy birthday with several bottles of wine, and he watched Merle gradually loosen up, as if she had been nervous of the event, although he couldn't fathom why. Perhaps she didn't want to go on a date with him? Perhaps it was too serious a gesture when they only had one day left with each other. But he could see she was enjoying herself.

He wished he could sit with her and talk about what he was feeling, but he knew it was out of the question. She mentioned her mother a couple of times during the evening, and each time, he saw her eyes lower as she remembered her responsibilities and felt the weight of her duty. There was no point in telling her he didn't want her to go. He knew she liked being with him, but she'd never had any plans for anything serious. What could they gain from saying anything else to each other? It would be like making plans for an invasion when you knew you didn't have the forces to fight.

The evening gradually came to an end and they had the tiramisu, the coffees and the liqueurs. Then it was time to go. Jake insisted on paying, as it was Neon's birthday treat, returning to the table as Merle left to visit the bathroom.

Neon watched her walk between the tables, the tight trousers framing her butt perfectly. He looked across, seeing Jake grinning at him. When he spoke, Jake's speech was slightly slurred. "So, do I owe you any money yet?"

Neon stared at him, not sure to what he was referring. Then he suddenly realised. The bet! He'd forgotten all about it. He glanced across at Bree, who was finishing off her brandy. "No..."

Bree put down the glass. "Money for what?"

Neon gave a slight shake of his head, but his cousin was too drunk to notice. "Neon bet me a hundred bucks he could get Merle to say she loves him before she goes back to England." He grinned. "I thought I'd lost, but now I'm beginning to think I stand a chance." He patted Neon's hand. "You've still got one day left though, mate."

Bree turned to stare at Neon. He shifted in his seat and frowned. "What?"

"So that's all this is to you? A bet?"

He glared back. "You can talk. How much do you owe Merle? Does she ring you every time we have sex? Are you keeping count?"

Bree reddened slightly and shot a fiery look at Jake, who had the grace to look ashamed. She looked back at Neon, angry now. "Merle's not even mentioned it to me."

"I saw her note to you, Bree, so get off your high horse." She glared at him and he sighed. "Don't let's argue. I'm glad you pushed her—otherwise I wouldn't have had so much fun over the last few days. But that's all it is—fun. We both know that. We're not under any illusions."

Bree studied him. "I hope she breaks your heart, Neon Carter, I really do."

He said nothing, seeing Merle coming out of the bathroom, and they stood, walking out to the two taxis waiting for them.

"Well, good night," said Jake awkwardly.

Bree looked at Neon. He sent her a pleading glance. *Don't tell her!* Her face softened and she came forward to kiss him on the cheek before turning to her sister and giving her a hug.

"Have a great day tomorrow." Bree's lips curled and she winked at Merle. "I hope you can walk at the end of it!"

Merle grinned back. "See you Friday morning."

They got into their separate taxis. Neon put his arm around Merle and she cuddled up to him as the car left the restaurant for the short drive to his house.

He thought about Bree's words to him. *I hope she breaks your heart, Neon Carter, I really do.* He'd never had a broken heart before. In fact, come to think of it, he'd never had a woman break up with him. It was always him who had done the breaking. He looked at Merle, her blonde head resting against his shoulder. Walking away from her on Friday was going to be the hardest thing he'd ever had to do.

Bree's words settled on him like a curse.

Chapter Thirteen

Even though the house was only five minutes from the restaurant, Merle was dozing by the time the taxi pulled up. Neon paid the driver and led her, sleepy and sighing, into the house and through to the bedroom.

"I've eaten so much I'm going to pop." She dropped her clothes on the floor and climbed into bed without further ado.

He smiled. "Why don't you get comfy? I want to get a glass of water."

She curled up in the bed, already half asleep. "Don't be long."

"I won't." He watched her eyes close before going back into the living room.

He hesitated in the kitchen, then got out the bottle of Laphroaig whisky he kept in the cupboard and poured himself a small glass. He went over to the window, looking out at the garden. It was dark outside, although there was nearly a full moon, its beams painting the bush with silver.

He took a swallow of the whisky, feeling Merle's presence in the house even though she was in another room, as a Geiger counter might pick up radioactivity. He liked having her there. He felt comfortable with her around. She didn't make any demands on him, she didn't keep asking where he was or following him around like a puppy. She was just there when he needed her, which was pretty much all the time, he had to admit, but that wasn't the point.

What was the point? He wasn't sure. He couldn't formulate his feelings into words. Probably the drink, he thought, looking into the glass, the thin layer of whisky coating the bottom. He wasn't a man used to having to think about this sort of thing. It was always the women who did the thinking, and he had to react to their declarations of love. But Merle hadn't said she loved him. She hadn't said anything to him, and somehow he knew she wouldn't.

There was nothing to be decided, no thoughts to formulate. On Friday, this whole episode would be over, and then he could get on with his life. Without her.

Finishing off the drink, resisting the urge to guzzle the rest of the bottle and numb his mind, he went into the bedroom and undressed, sliding in beside her. She'd turned over so her back was toward him, and he curled around her, pressing a light kiss on her cheek before settling down.

It was a while before sleep claimed him, though, and he lay there for ages, looking out into the darkness, the kiwis' mournful crying echoing his aching heart.

The next morning, he was awoken by a rustling noise and the brush of someone's lips on his. He opened his eyes to see Merle leaning over him.

She smiled. "Morning, sleepy."

"What's the time?"

"Eight thirty."

"Eight thirty!"

She rolled her eyes. "It's not quite lunchtime."

"I know, but I'm always awake by seven."

She laughed. "Must have been all the alcohol!" She sat back and he rolled onto his side to see her sitting there with his guitar.

"What's going on?"

She held up a finger, then placed her fingers on a C chord. Strumming, she sang "Happy Birthday to You", changing chords to G and F awkwardly, her tongue poking out of the side of her mouth each time, making him laugh when she hit a bum note but managing to get to the end of the song.

When she'd finished, he gave her a long kiss before saying, "Where did you learn that?"

"I found it online. I've been practising for half an hour."

He lay back, smiling. "Well, thank you, that's probably the nicest present I've ever had."

"Ah, but you haven't opened this yet." Her eyes gleamed. She handed him a package, about six inches square.

He stared at it, then looked back up at her. She wrinkled her nose at him. He tore off the paper and lifted the lid of the cardboard box. It was a mug.

He pulled it out and turned it around, then began laughing. He knew you could buy kits with a blank white mug and special pens to draw your message as he'd once got them for the kids in the family. She'd carefully drawn the seal of the President of the United States, the American eagle complete with olive branch in one talon and thirteen arrows in the other and the scroll in its mouth, and above it, she'd written *The West Wing*. He turned it around. On the other side, she'd written *What's Next?*

He studied it for a moment. What was she saying? Was she drawing attention to the fact that in a few days she'd be going back to England? That she would then be free to find another man to replace him? *What's Next?* More like *Who's Next?*

Her excited smile faded. "Don't you like it?" She tapped the writing. "I wasn't sure whether to write WWLD—What Would Leo Do, or what the President always says."

Realisation washed over him—she was referring to President Bartlet's favourite line. They'd actually joked about it the other day, saying it to each other after they'd made love—okay, done that, what's next? His throat tightened. "I love it." He forced a smile on his face. "Thank you."

"So polite," she teased, leaning forward to kiss him. "I got the kit from Bree. I did it the other day when you were working out."

He put his arms around her. "It's even better than the guitar playing."

"Well, duh." She kissed him again. "And now I'm going to make you a cup of coffee the way you like it." She leapt out of bed, completely naked. "You want any breakfast?"

"Not at the moment, thanks."

She looked surprised. "I don't think I've ever heard you turn down food."

He laughed. "Coffee would be great."

He watched her disappear and heard her singing in the kitchen as she ground the coffee and put it in the espresso machine, then foamed the milk. He lay back, thinking of how she'd sung to him and the time she'd taken to draw on the mug. She hadn't bought him an expensive present—there'd been no glamorous declarations of love, and yet he didn't think any woman had ever done anything so thoughtful for him.

He covered his face with his arm. His stomach was churning. Damn Bree and her stupid curse!

True to their word, the two of them stayed in bed all day and gradually worked their way through episodes of *The West Wing* on the TV in his bedroom, interspersed with various breaks for food, drinks, a swim in the pool and lazy bouts of lovemaking, sometimes even during episodes, when the mood arose.

Merle didn't think she'd ever had such a wonderful day. After the initial weird atmosphere when she'd given him her present, Neon had relaxed and returned to his normal mischievous self, playful and good-humoured, teasing and warm at the same time.

As they watched one of the episodes, curled up together, she wondered about the odd look that had appeared on his face when he'd opened the mug and studied her artwork. Had she overstepped the mark in buying him a present? She couldn't think why. She'd purposefully picked something lighthearted, although she had taken a long time doing the drawing. But it wasn't as if she'd bought him an expensive piece of jewellery, or one of those necklaces with a heart broken in the middle where you both wore a piece of it. And he had told her he expected a present, after all.

In the end, she decided not to worry about it. He'd put the mug next to his bed and she saw him glance at it occasionally. Maybe it had touched him more than she thought.

The phone rang several times during the day. Once it was Bree, wishing him happy birthday, then another member of his family, and the third time it was Julia. That had been an amusing call.

"Hi," he said when he heard who it was. They were lying in bed, the DVD paused, halfway through a tub of hokey-pokey honeycomb ice cream.

Merle heard Julia sing "Happy Birthday" down the phone to him and watched him roll his eyes, although he smiled afterward. "Thanks." He listened for a moment, then he glanced at her. "Yes, she's here." His eyes took on an exasperated look. "We're in bed." He grinned at Merle. "Well, you did ask. No, I've chained her to the headboard." Merle shook her head, alarmed. God, Julia must think she was such a slut. "Mum, I'm not wearing her out, more like the other way around." Merle whacked him with a pillow and he laughed. "She's giving me a bit of S and M now." Cheeks burning, she walked off into the kitchen, hearing his laughter echoing along the corridor.

He came out shortly afterward and went up to her where she was washing up the plates from lunch, putting his arms around her.

"Your mother must think I'm a complete hussy."

He laughed and kissed her head. "Hardly, she thinks you're good for me." He rested his lips on her hair and she stopped cleaning, her heart thumping. They said nothing for a moment. She closed her eyes momentarily. This was getting harder and harder. Every time she thought about walking away from him tomorrow, she got a pain in her chest.

She swallowed and finished washing up a glass, placing it in the rack. "Well, she can't mean food-wise. I don't think I've eaten anything healthy for the past week."

He kissed her ear. "Do you want some pasta for dinner?"

"That would be nice." She kept her tone light-hearted. "I'll cook for you. It is your birthday."

"Nope, I insist. It'll make a change. I normally only cook for one."

Merle smiled, wiping her hands on a cloth. She reached out and took his hand. "Why don't you come and play for me for a while."

She led him back into the bedroom and curled up on the bed as he took the guitar and began to play George Harrison's "All Things Must Pass". She sighed inwardly, wondering why he had chosen the song. She'd asked him to play because he usually looked happy when he was singing, but she sensed this time he was thinking more about the words than the music, his eyes surprisingly sad when he glanced up at her as he sang.

The rest of the day passed in much the same way, bittersweet, although they both made an effort to cover it. He made her some pasta, and they finally got dressed and sat outside in the warm sunshine to eat it, keeping the conversation light, talking about films and other series they'd watched and loved, and about their favourite periods of history—anything but the inevitable moment that was rapidly approaching.

As the day lengthened and the sun began to set, they went back to bed and made love, then curled up together, watching more *The West Wing*. A heaviness settled on her chest, her heart thumping each time she thought about leaving. But she continued to say nothing, knowing it was pointless and would only make it harder for them both when the moment finally came.

Eventually it was late and they were both drowsing, but neither of them could bring themselves to turn off the DVD, so they dozed, waking occasionally to see the episode had changed, until the titles came up and the DVD turned itself off.

Merle roused around one in the morning, saw the blue screen of the TV, and used the remote to turn it off. Then she curled around him, his arm settling on her waist even though he was asleep, and she lay there for ages until her eyelids descended again.

It was half past five when Neon finally woke properly, an hour before his alarm was due to go off. Merle was still asleep, and he lay there for a while, studying her, wondering whether he should leave her, as she looked so comfortable. Eventually, however, like a small boy faced with an open box of sweets, he couldn't resist starting to touch her, placing kisses on her cheeks, tracing light fingers over her skin.

She roused and looked up at him, smiling, her blue eyes hazy with sleep. "*Morena.*"

"*Morena,* sweetheart."

She blinked sleep away, then looked at the clock. "Do you have to get up?"

"Not yet. Go back to sleep if you want."

She started to smile. "I can't while you're doing that." His fingers were circling her breasts.

"Turn over. Then I won't be tempted."

She did so, her lips curling, closing her eyes and sighing as he continued to trace his fingers across her back, following the line of her waist, skimming her hips, brushing up her spine. He caressed her for ages, drawing korus and other patterns across her skin, joining up her moles, telling her they made a picture of Winston Churchill, which made her laugh.

Then he started writing his name with his finger, over and over, all down her back, on her arms, her hips.

"Are you worried I'm going to call out the wrong name or something?"

He didn't laugh. "I'm branding you."

"Like a cow?"

"I'm making sure you never forget me. This will always be here, like a tattoo."

She caught her breath. His fingers laced the letters of his name in thick capitals, then in handwriting, then in copperplate with loops and swirls, then in French, with the accent on the *e*. His fingers felt hot, almost as if he had been speaking the truth and he really was searing the letters into her skin. Unbidden, tears came into her eyes. She bit her lip, making sure they didn't form. She didn't want to give him a reason to be impatient or irritated as he had been with Ella at the end.

He turned her onto her back and looked at her searchingly. She forced her lips into a smile, reached up and brushed the hair from his forehead. "I won't forget you, Napoleon Carter."

He didn't even comment on her use of his full name. "I'll make sure you don't." His hand brushed her body, starting to caress her. "Every time you make love to another guy, I want you to think of me."

He lowered his lips to kiss her. She accepted it, fighting the urge to push him away. It was such a cruel, arrogant thing to say, particularly because she knew it was now extremely unlikely she'd ever be able to sleep with another man. This was it. When she returned to England, she would throw herself into her work, into looking after her mother, and she would never date again. She couldn't bear the thought of someone else touching her. At that moment, she loved him desperately, had fallen deeply in love with him, like Ella and probably all the women before her.

She wanted to hate him for his words, and yet she couldn't blame him because it was exactly how she felt too. Some part of her hoped when she was gone, he would ache with longing for her and be unable to sleep with anyone else. Somehow, though, she knew it wouldn't be the same for him. There would be other women—soon, knowing his sex drive—and, one day, eventually, he would forget her. He would assume it couldn't have been as good as he imagined. He would get married and have children,

161

and she would be a distant memory, a nostalgic reminiscence at Christmastime. He might swim in the pool or watch *The West Wing*, think briefly of her and smile.

She bit her lip hard as he started kissing her body, tracing his tongue down her skin. She mustn't think about anything other than this moment, this second. She had to live in the present and make the most of being there with him. It wasn't his fault. He hadn't promised her anything. She'd known what he was like when she first slept with him. Bree had told her before she even met him, "His middle name's 'Feral'."

His words just now had been of the moment, a passionate statement, like telling someone you love them when you're drunk. He didn't mean it. He was trying to let her know he was enjoying the time they were having.

So, she let him make love to her slowly, very slowly. He spent ages covering her with kisses, licking every inch of her skin, tasting her, touching her, as if he wanted to commit every little freckle, every hair to memory. He made her turn over so he could do the same to her back, tracing kisses along her legs, then up, before turning her onto her back again and eventually moving up to her face, taking a long time to kiss her properly, deep, languorous kisses, brushing her tongue with his, until she was sighing, her body desperate for him.

Eventually he gave in and lay on top of her, nudging her legs apart to slide into her. He moved gently, pausing in between each thrust to kiss her, demanding she keep her eyes open, as if he also wanted to brand himself on the back of her retinas, forcing her to see him when she shut her eyes, like looking into a camera flash.

As she came, she thought she saw a glimmer of moisture in his eyes, but then he smiled and it was gone. As he joined in with his own climax, she clutched hold of him, knowing it would be the last time, feeling the knowledge deep inside her, almost unbearable, wishing she could freeze time and make the moment last forever.

Chapter Fourteen

Afterward, it was time for him to get ready for work. He showered, then she went into the bathroom while he got dressed. When she came out, he was standing by the window, staring out at the heavy tropical rain that had started to fall, pooling on the deck. She studied him for a moment without moving. He'd pulled on jeans but had yet to don a T-shirt, and her gaze lingered on his muscles and the beautiful curling tattoo, and she smiled as she thought about how she'd traced it with her tongue.

Then she thought about the fact that she had merely minutes left with him. Four whole days and nights they'd shared, and now they were over. For a moment, she was tempted to ask whether he'd like to meet up after he finished work the next day—the night before she flew back. But they'd agreed on the timeline—he'd mentioned the four days right from the beginning, and she didn't want to plead for extra time.

He turned and looked over at her, but she didn't say anything. Her throat tightened, but she was determined not to make a fuss. She made herself think of Ella, of the look on his face when he'd spoken to her on the phone that day, impatient, irritated. She didn't want him to look like that because of her.

She smiled, and he smiled back, well mannered as strangers. She slipped on her skirt and top as he found a shirt, and went back into the bathroom to gather her few items, bringing them out and stuffing them in her bag. She brushed her hair rapidly and caught it up with a clip. Her heart was pounding, and she felt suddenly sick.

He cleared his throat. "Do you want a cup of something before you go?"

"No, I'm fine, thanks." She couldn't have forced any food or drink past her lips.

"Okay." He pulled on socks and shoes. She finished packing her bag. They completed the tasks in silence.

When they were both ready, he locked the doors to the decking. Then it was time to go.

Merle's stomach churned, but she kept the emotion from her face. She would *not* let him see her cry. She would not be one of the women he talked about to his mates, who always asked too much of him, who weren't happy with just sex. She wanted him to have fond memories of her. To think of her, maybe every little while, with a smile.

She walked out to the car, leaving him to lock the front door, and climbed in, her heart pounding. He joined her and started the car, heading it up the drive, past the orange trees. She had to use all her inner strength not to turn around and look longingly back at the house, at the beautiful pool she would never see again.

They drove in silence to Bree's house and pulled into the drive. He put the car into park but left the engine running. She got the message. He didn't want to wait and draw out the goodbye.

She turned to face him, her heart thumping. She made herself smile, her eyes warm. "Have a good day."

He nodded. His fingers tapped on the wheel. "You too."

She bit her lip. Wasn't he going to say anything? "We had a good time, didn't we?"

For the first time he smiled, the corners of his eyes crinkling. "Yes. We did."

"Thank you for a great four days, Neon. I've had such fun."

"Me too."

"Thanks for letting me stay at your house. Although I guess it was like showing a captured spy the plans for an invasion, knowing they're going to be shot the next day."

He started laughing. "That wasn't quite what I had in mind."

She grinned. That was how she wanted to remember him, laughing, a teasing light in his eyes. She bent forward and kissed him quickly, lingering ever so slightly, then pulled back and got out of the car. There was nothing more to be said. She ran over to the house and let herself in, not looking back.

Inside, she leaned against the door, waiting. For a moment, there was no sound. Then she heard the engine rev and the scrunch of tyres on gravel. The car went down the drive, and she heard it disappear up the main road.

Footsteps came along the hall and Bree appeared, rubbing her eyes. "Oh hi! You're early!" She stopped, looking at Merle's face. "Are you okay?"

"Fine," said Merle. Then she pressed a hand to her mouth and burst into tears.

Bree led her to the kitchen table and made her a cup of tea, then sat beside her and handed her tissues as she made Merle tell her what had happened.

"I should have known it was a bad idea, you staying there." She sighed as Merle wiped away the tears, only to have more take their place.

"It wasn't your fault." Merle sniffed. "I only had myself to blame. I shouldn't have stayed, but I couldn't say no. We had such a good time, I thought..."

"What?"

"I thought he... I don't know."

"Loved you?"

"Maybe." She wiped her face again and tried to smile. "Stupid, eh? I've only known him for a week."

Bree studied her. "I think he does love you, in his own, crazy, anti-commitment way. It certainly showed in his eyes the other day at the restaurant. But Merle, even if he does, did you think he'd say it? He knows you're going away. He knows your life is in England, that you would never leave Mum. I mean, it was never going to work, was it?"

"I know, I know..." Merle put her face in her hands and drew a long, shaky sigh. "God, I'm so stupid..."

"You're not stupid, you're in love."

Merle looked up. Jake had appeared, hands in his pockets.

Merle blinked at her. "In love?"

"Well, duh." Bree rolled her eyes. "Did you tell him you loved him?"

"No. I wouldn't have done that. I saw how he was when he was on the phone to Ella. He hated it. I wasn't going to do that to him."

Bree glanced at Jake, who turned and walked out of the room. She sighed, frowning. "What a bloody, complicated mess. I'm to blame for introducing you in the first place and putting that stupid idea in your head about sleeping with someone. I never thought it would lead to this."

"I'll be okay. I'm sorry to turn up on your doorstep like this.

167

But I will get over him. It was a shock this morning, it was horrible leaving him, that's all. I'll be fine."

Merle spent the morning curled up on the sofa, watching TV, her gaze drifting to the rain outside. She couldn't stop thinking about what Neon was doing. Was he out on a call or sitting in the station, doing paperwork? Was he thinking of her at all?

She didn't want any lunch. Bree fussed around her, bringing her drinks. When Jake went into town, Bree decided to stay behind. Merle didn't object. She didn't want to be alone.

When Jake came back, Merle heard him discussing something in the kitchen with Bree. She sat up. Bree was watching her, brow furrowed. "What's up?"

"Nothing." Bree smiled.

"Bree... I'm not stupid."

Her sister sighed. Jake came over and kissed the top of Merle's head. "The fire alarm went off while I was in town. All the engines are out and so are all the ambulances from St John's. It must be quite a big emergency."

Merle's eyes met Bree's. She swallowed. "Would he have gone out with them?"

Jake nodded. "Probably. But he'll be fine, Merle. He plays more of an observing role now. He won't be on the front line."

She said nothing, lying back on the sofa, watching the rain again. It was ridiculous to be worried. He wasn't her man. He wasn't hers to worry about. And it was his job, for Christ's sake. He knew what he was doing.

Three hours went by, and it was still raining. Merle read a magazine and watched a chat show, although she couldn't have told Bree anything about either of them. Then she went into the bedroom and lay on the bed, looking out at the sodden garden, the dripping palms. She felt knotted inside, and her head was spinning. She wished she were flying back to the UK that night. Not because she wanted to leave New Zealand—she ached at the thought. And it wasn't just because of Neon. She had grown to love the country, and it was going to be difficult to say goodbye to her sister. But she thought she had an inkling of how it might feel to be someone who was about to be beheaded at the Tower. You always hoped for a last-minute reprieve, but deep down you knew it wasn't going to happen, and in the end, you wanted to step up to the block and feel the cold blade on your neck and know it was all over.

There was a knock at the front door. Merle stiffened and walked into the living room to hover in the doorway, meeting Jake's eyes where he sat in the chair, reading. She heard voices, and Bree appeared with Julia close behind.

Julia stopped when she saw Merle, smiled, came over and kissed her on the cheek. "Hello, Merle."

"Hi, Julia."

Neon's mother followed Bree to the sofa and sat. Merle hesitated, then perched on the arm of one of the chairs.

"I've heard from Neon," said Julia. "He gave me a quick ring and I thought you might want to know what's going on."

Jake nodded. "I heard the sirens."

"There's been an accident on State Highway Ten at Bulls Gorge. A busload of tourists crashed. They think it was due to the bad weather. It veered off the road, taking a couple of cars with it and rolled, and it's now upside down."

"Oh no." Both Merle and Bree covered their mouths.

"The bus was full. The driver of one of the cars is dead, and a couple of the bus passengers have died. They've got most of the passengers out, but there's some problem with the last section of the bus. Something's collapsed or been crushed, and they're trapped. And there are children in there."

Merle stood and walked over to the window, her arms wrapped around her body, looking out at the rain. She stayed there as the others discussed the accident, her mind whirling, thinking of Neon out there in this awful weather, trying to deal with such a horrendous event. Part of her felt a swell of pride. He would be calm and organised, and would do his utmost to get everyone out safely. Hopefully he would look after himself and not take any unnecessary risks. She turned as Julia spoke.

"Would you mind if I stayed here for a bit?" Julia said. "Pierre's gone to Auckland and the house is so quiet!"

Bree leaned over and kissed her. "Of course not. I'll put the kettle on."

Merle continued to look out at the rain as she heard Bree bustling around in the kitchen. After a few minutes, she felt a presence at her side and turned to see Julia standing there, looking at her.

"Are you okay?" Julia said. "You look very pale."

Merle nodded, touched Julia had asked. "I'm fine, thank you."

Julia's eyes were wide and brown, very like her son's. "Did you say goodbye this morning?"

Merle nodded. Unbidden, a rush of tears came into her eyes, and she bit her lip hard, turning her head. Julia sighed, came up and put her arm around her. Merle couldn't stop a tear falling down her cheek, and she cursed as she wiped it away. "Sorry," she said, giving a small smile. "You must have to do this with a lot of Neon's girls."

Julia gave her a funny look. "Sweetheart, you're not just one of his 'girls'. I assumed you knew that."

Merle frowned. "Thank you for being so sweet. But we both knew it was just a quick fling when we got together."

Julia studied Merle, her face expressionless. "What did he say to you this morning?"

Merle blinked, wiping away another tear, annoyed with herself. "He didn't say anything. I didn't expect him to, Julia."

Julia turned and looked out of the window. She gave a small, ironic laugh. "My son's an idiot." Her eyes came back to Merle's, and she sighed, but she didn't say any more.

At that moment, Bree brought over two mugs of tea, and Julia took hers and sat. Merle sipped hers, wondering what Julia had meant. She would probably never find out. She looked out at the rain. Tomorrow she would be out of here, and maybe then she could get on with her life.

Another hour and a half went by. Bree prepared some tea, and they all nibbled—apart from Jake whose appetite was almost as big as Neon's—and tried to watch TV.

They paid more attention when the news finally came on. The accident was the third story, and there were already camera crews there. The four of them sat on the edge of their seats as they saw the scene from a helicopter, gasping at the sight of the bus crumpled at the base of the bank. The camera cut to a reporter, who stood with a firefighter on the edge of the scene.

"This is Chief Fire Officer John Wright. He's been here since this morning, and he's going to give us an update on what's happening with the passengers still trapped in the bus." The reporter held the microphone to the CFO.

"We're currently in the process of trying to get the last few people out of the bus," Wright said. "We're working against the clock. The section is right above the fuel tank. We're worried about the bus catching fire."

"How many people are in there?"

"Four, as far as we can make out. One man, one woman, and two children. We've already pulled the children's mother out, and she's unconscious. An ambulance took her to hospital. The two children are conscious and very frightened."

"So what's stopping you getting to them?"

"The bus has been crushed, and we're trying to cut through the metal, but it's taking longer than we thought, and we're now worried about the risk of fire. My SSO has volunteered to try and crawl in the gap we've managed to make and get them out, but it's not going to be easy."

In the living room, the four of them looked at each other. Merle blinked. SSO? Senior station officer?

The reporter pressed her hand to her ear, then turned toward the bus. "I'm hearing there's movement in the bus. Yes, I can see a hand coming out the side there—it's one of the children, a little girl by the looks of it, she's coming out, she looks okay, she's moving..." The camera captured the firefighters pulling out the little girl and transferring her to the waiting ambulance.

The reporter craned her neck. "Here comes someone else, it's a woman, she's out, she looks okay—and here's another person, yes it's the man, that leaves the other child, he's the only one left inside..."

At that moment, there was a bang on the TV and shouts echoed from the upturned bus. Fire roared, and smoke billowed into the rain. "Excuse me," said the CFO, running down the hill.

"Oh no." Julia sat with both hands over her mouth. Merle watched, horrified.

"The bus has caught fire," said the reporter, "and we know there's a firefighter inside, trying to get the remaining passenger out." The camera captured the scene, with the firefighters

172

pouring water onto the fire, others bending by the side of the gap, trying to reach inside.

Merle's heart was pounding. This was too horrible. Poor Julia. Neon's mum sat with her gaze fixed on the screen, tears pouring down her face. Merle went over and sat beside her, putting an arm around her.

The reporter was narrating the event. "There's no sign of movement yet, we know there's a child inside with the firefighter. The smoke's starting to billow out now, and the fire's raging, in spite of the rain. No, hold on, I can see movement. The other firefighters are reaching in for something, yes, they've got a figure, I can see them cradling a head—it's the other child, the boy, but he's not moving—they're pulling him out of the window now, straight onto a stretcher, and they are transferring him to an ambulance, but he's not moving." The camera went back to the bus. "And there's the firefighter, look. He's coming through the window. They're pulling him out—he looks okay. Goodness, what tension here in the Northland." The camera swung back to the reporter. "Well, it looks like everyone's finally out of the bus, so it's back to you in the studio and we'll give you an update shortly when we know more."

Julia stood and went over to the window again, brushing her face. Merle followed her and put her arms around her. "It's okay, he's all right, we saw him get out, he's going to be okay..."

"I know." Julia leaned her head on Merle's shoulder. "It's so awful. I can't bear to think what he has to go through. Why does he have to volunteer for everything?"

Merle stroked her hair, tears pouring down her own face. "He'll be all right. He's made of stern stuff. And he loves his job, Julia, this is what he wants to do, he wants to be on the front line. It's what makes him the man he is. You've done such a good job bringing him up. He wouldn't be the man he is without you."

Julia sniffed, then gave a little laugh. "That's a nice thing to say. Thank you."

Merle laughed back, wiping her face. "You're very welcome. And how much would he love this, eh? All of us crying over him?"

"For God's sake, don't tell him," said Bree, brushing away her own tears.

They sat back on the sofa, talking about the accident and drinking tea for another hour and a half before Julia's mobile finally rang. It was nearly eight o'clock by then, two and a half hours after Neon's shift should have finished. Julia jumped, grabbed the phone from the table and flipped it up.

Chapter Fifteen

"Hello?" Julia looked at the other three and nodded. "Hello, darling, how are you, are you all right? We saw you on TV, the accident was on the news. You gave us quite a fright. How's the last child? Oh. At Whangarei? And their mother? Well, that's something at least. Where are you now? It's nearly eight. Okay. No, you go, thanks for calling, I'll see you later." She hung up. "He had to go, the CFO was calling him." She gave a big sigh. "He sounds okay, very tired. The child is unconscious, but he is alive. He's in intensive care. The mother's come around though, which is something. The fire's out, so they're coming back for the night now. He'll be at the station in twenty minutes."

Merle sipped her tea, although she had to force herself to swallow. Her relief was so strong she felt faint.

Julia looked over at Merle. "Would you go to the station and meet him?"

Merle stared at her. "Me?" She gave a wry laugh. "I'm the last person he'd want to see. You should go, or Jake."

Julia shook her head. "I know he'd want to see you. He should have someone with him tonight."

"We said goodbye this morning. He's not going to want to see me again, especially tonight. He'll be exhausted, he'll want to get home and sleep."

"I know my son better than he knows himself at times. He'll

want to see you."

Merle looked from her to Bree and Jake, open mouthed. She was desperate to see him, to make sure he was all right, but how could she put herself through it all again after saying goodbye that morning? "I'm sorry... I can't..."

"Please?"

Merle bit her lip. Bree reached out and touched her hand. "Why don't you go, Merle? Jake will run you down. Be there for him as a friend. Look after him, make sure he has something to eat, give him a drink, put him to bed. Then you can give us a ring and we'll pick you up. But I think Julia's right. He would love to see you."

Merle wasn't so sure. But Julia's face was so pleading in the end she said, "Okay, I'll go."

"Thank you." Julia gave her a hug. "I'll ring in the morning. Let me know if there's anything he needs before then."

Merle nodded. She went into the bedroom and quickly shoved a couple of things in her bag. She wasn't sure if Neon would want to see her. She was certain he'd been as relieved as she had when they'd finally parted. Now they would only have to go through it all again. If he even asked her to go home with him, which she doubted would happen.

Her heart thudded at the thought of seeing him. She took her bag into the living room and said goodbye to Julia and Bree, promising to ring them if she had any news. Julia wrote her mobile and home numbers on a scrap of paper, and Merle put them in her bag. Jake was waiting with his car keys, so they went out and got in the car and waved goodbye to Bree and Julia before heading down the road.

It was still light, the rain finally easing a little, the channels at the side of the road heavy with rushing water.

"You okay?" Jake asked.

Merle nodded. She was so nervous her mouth had gone dry. "Will you stay till he turns up, in case he doesn't want to see me?"

Jake laughed. "Sure. But it's not going to happen."

"Everyone's so sure," Merle murmured. "Except me."

Jake pulled up in the public car park by the fire station. Two engines were already back. Firefighters were climbing down, their faces tired and dirty. Merle and Jake walked up to the entrance. She paused there, her heart hammering, searching for Neon's face. Had he returned yet?

Then she saw him talking to another firefighter at the other side of the entrance. He'd taken off his helmet, which was under his arm, but was still wearing his uniform. At any other time, Merle would have fainted from lust. He looked huge in the sandy-coloured coveralls with yellow reflective banding, the collar standing up around his neck, black gloves in his hand. Now, however, she saw the sooty streaks across his uniform, the black marks and scratches on his tired face. His hair was ruffled and sticking up, and her heart went out to him. She took a step forward and stopped, unsure whether he would want to see her.

The man he was talking to glanced over and saw her staring at him. He smiled, nudged Neon and nodded toward her. Neon turned and looked over, his gaze settling on her. For a moment, he just stared. She tried to smile but couldn't, she was completely frozen on the spot. *Please don't let him turn away.* If he did, she would walk right out and get back in Jake's car.

Not taking his eyes from her, Neon shoved his gloves and helmet into the hands of the firefighter he'd been talking to and crossed the short distance between them. Without saying a word, he walked straight up to her and enfolded her tightly in his arms.

Merle put her arms around his waist, conscious of the soot and the acrid smell of smoke but not caring a bit, pressing herself up to him. His arms were so tight, she thought he might crack a rib, but she didn't say anything, so glad he hadn't turned away. He didn't kiss her, didn't say anything, just stood there inhaling her hair, absorbing her presence.

Eventually one of the other firefighters whistled, and Neon pulled back, casting a wry glance over his shoulder before looking at her. Jake gave him a slap on the shoulder. "Good to see you're okay. Can I leave her with you?"

She looked up at Neon, seeing for the first time the cuts and bruises on his face and the blood on his neck. Was it his? He was frowning. Was he wondering how to say no? He cleared his throat. "I need to write my report. It might take a while."

The firefighter he'd been talking to, whom Merle now recognised as the chief fire officer who'd been interviewed on the TV, now came up to them. "Not now, son. Go home. Do it in the morning."

Sighing, Neon nodded, and Jake kissed her on the cheek. "Call me if you want picking up at all." After retrieving her bag, he walked off, leaving them alone.

Neon studied her. She hadn't seen him look this tired before. He was usually brimming with energy. He indicated his uniform. "I need to get out of this. Do you mind waiting?"

"Of course not." She watched him walk off into the station.

"You must be Merle." She turned to see John Wright smiling at her. "I've heard a lot about you."

"Good things, I hope." She smiled. "I saw you on the news. That was a great job you did today."

"Oh, I didn't do anything. It's the guys who get in the thick of it who are the real heroes."

"I thought the SSOs were supposed to be a supervisory role," she said wryly, looking after Neon.

He laughed. "There'll be snow in Kerikeri before I manage to keep him out of the action. That's a good man you've got there, love. Hang on to him."

She smiled but didn't say anything. She knew Neon was a good man. But he wasn't hers to hang on to.

He came walking out of the station, dressed in the shirt and jeans he'd put on that morning, carrying his car keys. He shook Wright's hand before he left. "Good job today."

Wright smiled at him. "Nice work, Carter. If I hear anything about the boy, I'll give you a call."

"Sure."

They walked back to his car, in the Fire Emergency Services parking beside the station. "Do you want me to drive?" she asked.

"Sure."

She took the keys, opened the door and slid into the car. It was an automatic, and she had no problem working out the controls. He got in and clipped himself in tiredly, then leaned back, his head on the rest. She reversed out and drove carefully to his house.

They didn't speak on the way. Merle felt surprisingly calm. Her nerves had dissipated the moment he took her in his arms. Nothing had changed—she was still flying out in two days, their situation was the same. But he'd been pleased to see her there. This was a day out of days, like the eye of a tornado, a moment they'd been able to snatch, and she wasn't there for anything except to make sure he was all right. She loved him, and she was pretty sure he loved her, although they couldn't put it into words.

She pulled up outside his house and walked around to his side of the car, took his hand and led him indoors. She dropped her bag on the sofa and closed the curtains. Then she came back over to him. He stood there, hands on hips, staring at the floor. He looked so tired and so completely, utterly sad, she wanted to cry.

"Come on." She took his hand again and led him into the bedroom and through to the bathroom. "You're going to have a hot shower and a sandwich and a glass of whisky, or two, and then you're going to bed."

He followed her like a child and stood there while she turned on the spray. She bullied him out of his clothes, frowning as she saw the blood down the side of his face and on his neck. "Are you hurt badly?"

"It's only a scratch."

She knew better than to say he needed to see a doctor. She tested the water, making sure it was hot, and pushed him inside. "I'll make you a sandwich. I'll be back in five minutes."

"Okay." He stood under the hot shower, both hands on the tiles in front of him, letting the water run over his head.

She went out and immediately phoned Julia from the number in her bag. "It's only Merle," she said when his mum answered. "I wanted to let you know he's okay. Tired and a bit bruised and battered, but he's in one piece."

"Thank you, darling. Are you staying the night?"

"I...don't know yet. Maybe. I'll see what he wants. I'm going to make him a sandwich."

Julia laughed. Then she said, "But he was pleased to see you?"

Merle smiled. "Yes, you were right."

"Look after him, Merle."

"I will. I'll speak to you tomorrow."

"Good night."

Merle hung up and went into the kitchen. She made him a sandwich, filled a glass with milk to go with it and took it into the bedroom. Going back into the kitchen, she found the bottle of whisky and poured a generous measure into a whisky glass, throwing in a couple of ice cubes for good measure. She took that into the bedroom too, left it on the bedside table, and went into the bathroom.

The room was full of steam. He was still in the same pose, hands on the tiles, head under the shower, grey soot and blood mixing in the water by his feet, and she realised he hadn't moved at all. He turned his head slightly and she saw him register her presence, but he didn't meet her eyes.

She studied him for a moment, seeing the black streaks on his face and hands, the blood on his neck. She caught the bottom of her T-shirt, lifting it over her head, then took off her skirt. She walked up to the shower cabinet, opened the door and stepped in.

He moved his head but didn't look at her. "Merle..."

"Ssh." She got the sponge and squeezed some shower gel on it. "I'm here as a friend, Neon. I'm not going anywhere. Deal with it."

He gave a wry laugh but didn't say anything. She lathered up the sponge and started washing him, and he sighed, letting her, wincing occasionally as she touched a tender spot. As she gradually cleared the soot off, she realised how hurt he was. Something had fallen across his ribs, leaving bruises already starting to go purple, and his shoulders were red with scrapes and gashes.

"What happened here?" She sponged them gently.

"There was a plate of metal in the way. I was lying on my front and I couldn't turn around, otherwise I'd have kicked it in. I had to shoulder it down."

She touched the red marks, frowning. "You should have waited for some help."

"There wasn't time, or space. I was the only thing between them and that fire."

She squeezed out the sponge, put more gel on, lathered it up and started on the other side. "You did well today, Neon. You saved the lives of all those people stuck in that bus."

He moved his foot around on the floor, washing the blood into the plughole. "The boy's still unconscious."

"But he's alive. He wouldn't be, if it wasn't for you."

He didn't say anything. She continued to wash him down, cleaning his face and finally his neck, realising the blood was coming from a gash below his chin. "You should have stitches in that."

"I'll get a bandage."

She didn't say anything. Turning off the shower, she stepped out and got some fresh towels. She rolled up a wad of toilet paper and pressed it against his neck, getting him to hold it there, then dried him quickly. He watched her, amused now, but didn't say anything. Eventually she gave him the towel. "Wait there. I'll find something to put on that wound."

"There's a first-aid box under the sink."

"Okay." She went out, still wet herself, and searched in the box, finding a large wound dressing and some antiseptic wipes, and bringing them back. He'd slipped on a thin towelling robe and was peeling off the tissue, looking in the mirror. "Here." She cleaned the wound and smoothed on the dressing.

"Thanks."

"Go and get in bed. And eat that sandwich."

"Yes, Mum."

She smiled, watching him go out, and quickly dried herself. Coming out, she rummaged in his wardrobe. "Can I put one of your T-shirts on? I left my robe at Bree's."

"Sure."

She pulled out an All Blacks tee and yanked it on, smiling as it dropped to her mid-thigh and elbows, then climbed onto the bed where he was half-sitting, half-lying against the pillows. She'd wondered if he'd say he was too tired to eat, but he'd already nearly finished the sandwich and now polished it off, licking his fingers. He pointed to her top. "Suits you."

She smiled, sitting beside him cross-legged, watching as he drank the whole glass of milk in one go. "Better?"

He sighed, leaning his head back against the pillows. "Yes, thanks."

"Good."

He took the glass of whisky and drank a large mouthful, then put his head back again. "I haven't eaten anything since lunch. Didn't realise how hungry I was."

"Do you want me to cook you a meal?"

He smiled and turned his head to look at her. "No, thanks, that was just right."

They studied each other for a moment. His beautiful brown eyes were dark with exhaustion. Eventually she said, "I rang your mum, by the way, to let her know you're okay."

"Thanks."

"No worries."

He smiled, then sipped his whisky. He held out his hand and she slipped hers into it, and he linked their fingers. He still looked incredibly sad.

"Do you want to talk about it?"

He looked at their hands, studied her fingers for a while. Finally, taking her completely by surprise, he said, "Do you want kids, Merle?"

She couldn't think what to say. She wanted to tell him, *Only with you.* But she knew she couldn't. Getting pregnant with his baby, giving birth to his children... That honour was going to go to another woman. It made her want to cry. Eventually she said, "Maybe. Do you?"

She expected him to give a vehement *No*, to say after today he never wanted to see another child again, but for a while he didn't say anything. He studied her hands, although she had a feeling he was seeing something else in his mind's eye.

He sipped the whisky again. "I'd not thought about it before. I've seen other people with children, watched them be so protective, so defensive of them, even when they're annoying little brats. I never understood before. You see people crying over starving kids in Africa, and Mum always gets tearful when she hears of children being mistreated, but I never saw them as anything other than young adults, if you know what I mean."

"Sort of." She smiled.

"I know it sounds stupid but I never understood why they needed special treatment, why, on the *Titanic*, it was women and children first. I mean I've been brought up to believe that's what you do, as a male, but I never *understood* why."

"But that changed today."

He nodded. "There were five people caught in the bus. Three adults and two kids."

"Yes, I saw the news."

"We got the kids' mother out but had to cut a hole in the side by the window to access the others. There was just enough room to squeeze through. We couldn't make it any bigger because the bus had compacted and there was too much metal to cut through—we knew the petrol tank was going to catch fire any minute."

"Why did you volunteer? I thought you weren't supposed to be the first in any more."

He met her eyes, then looked away. He stared at the glass in his hand and swirled the amber liquid around the ice. "After we cut the hole," he said, ignoring her question, "I went in and got hold of the little girl..." He took a sip of the whisky.

Merle waited patiently, puzzled. She knew he must have gone on hundreds of jobs during his career. But something had affected him tonight, more than usual, and she hoped he'd be able to open up to her and let her help him.

Chapter Sixteen

"She was crying, but she was okay, I could see she wasn't injured. She'd managed to undo her seat belt, you see, and had crawled forward, but her brother...he couldn't get his seat belt undone, he was only four years old..." His stopped again, sipped his whisky.

Tears stung Merle's eyes as he struggled to tell her what had happened. "Where was he?"

"Behind the others. The girl didn't want to leave him, but I made her come with me. I tried to be comforting and reassuring, but she kept crying, so I yelled at her." His eyes met hers briefly, then he looked away.

"You only did what you had to." She squeezed his hand.

He shrugged. "Eventually she came with me and I got her out and went back for the other two adults. I had to get them out first because they were blocking the way to the boy. He was screaming..." He stopped, cleared his throat. "I crawled through the bus—it was upside down, remember. I reached him and realised he'd twisted himself in the seat belt trying to right himself and it had locked. It wouldn't release. It was getting tighter and tighter. He was so frightened. I was about to cut him free when the tank exploded."

Merle's face was wet, but she hardly noticed.

"The sound was deafening, and the blast knocked him out.

There was smoke everywhere. I shared my BA—sorry, that's my breathing apparatus—with him, but I wasn't sure if he was breathing, and there wasn't time to give him first aid. I cut him loose and dragged him out—that's when I realised there was a sheet of metal blocking the way and I had to shoulder it down. I started to panic. I could see the fire at the end, and for a while, the blockage wouldn't budge. But eventually I got through, and a couple of the guys were waiting there to pull him out." He sipped the whisky again. "Apparently he's alive, but he's got a serious head injury where he was knocked out in the blast."

"At least he's alive," she reminded him again. "Completely due to you, Neon."

"If only I'd been quicker, got him out sooner..."

"Sweetheart, you did your best, you can't do more than that."

He shook his head. "He was so frightened, but when he saw me, he reached out for me. He kept calling me 'Fireman Sam'. He knew who I was, see, he knew I was there to rescue him. I feel so bad, Merle, I didn't do it in time, and I keep thinking, if I feel this bad and it's someone else's child, how much worse would it be if it were mine? You'd want to protect your kids from the world but you can't, you know?" He gave a harsh laugh. "Twenty-eight, and I'm only just beginning to understand the bond between a parent and child. How pathetic is that."

Tears were pouring down her face now, but she brushed them aside and got to her knees, leaning forward to kiss him on his lips, his cheeks. "Neon, you're the bravest man I know. You did everything you could to save that little boy, and he'll be able to thank you himself. I know he's going to be okay, he'll pull through." She put her arms around him. "One day, you'll meet the right woman, and you'll get married. You'll have kids of your own, and you'll be such a great dad—you'll be able to read

Fireman Sam stories to them, and take them for rides in the fire engine, and they'll be able to wear your hat..." He gave a short laugh and she smiled, cupping his face, although she thought her heart was going to splinter in two. "You're tired now, and it's been a hell of a day. You just need some sleep."

He looked up, his gaze meeting hers, and she caught her breath. His eyes glistened with unshed tears like two disks of polished mahogany left out in the rain. He looked so sad, and she still wasn't sure why.

He let out a shaky breath. "I won't be able to sleep. I keep hearing him screaming in my head. It won't go away." His voice broke, and he tipped his head back, bringing his arm up across his face, breathing heavily.

Neon was so tired he could sleep for a fortnight, but he knew he wasn't going to be able to close his eyes with the little boy's cries echoing in his head.

Truth to tell, though, that wasn't the only reason he was feeling like he'd been hollowed out with a spoon. When Merle had asked him earlier why he'd volunteered to go into the bus, he hadn't been able to tell her he'd done it because he wanted to place himself in danger, was even hoping something bad might happen to him, so it might distract him from the pain he was feeling inside.

Now he lay back on the bed, knowing she was there for him, and it was like the best moment and the worst moment of his life rolled into one. When he'd seen her standing in the entrance to the station, for a moment he'd thought he was dreaming. When he saw the hesitation in her eyes and realised she actually was there, relief had flooded through him that he wasn't going to have to go home alone.

Now, though, he wondered if he had been wise agreeing to

bring her back with him. They'd done the difficult parting, harsh as it had been, and now he was going to have to do it all again.

He let his arm drop, knowing his eyes were wet, unable to meet her gaze. He needed another drink. The only way he was going to be able to get through this night was to immerse himself in alcohol, but he didn't know if he could bring himself to walk to the kitchen. He could ask Merle to get him a drink. She'd said in the shower she was there as a friend, and he knew she'd do it for him. His mother had probably sent her. Somehow, Julia knew Merle was special to him. But what was she trying to achieve by it? No good could come of this night, none at all.

It was starting to get dark, but they hadn't put on any lamps, and the room had subsided into semidarkness. Merle had been studying him quietly, and now she leaned forward and kissed his chest, placing her lips lightly across the bruises on his rib cage, caused when the exploding tank had thrown him against the seats. He sighed, knowing he would be no good to her tonight, but too tired to do anything other than lie there and accept her gentle touch, so soft against his skin. He closed his eyes, but instantly he could see the inside of the bus, the frightened faces of the children, and hear the bang of the explosion and the billow of the smoke, grey and thick as a blanket. He'd had his breathing apparatus on, but he'd still been able to smell the acrid stench as it rolled over him.

His eyes flew open and he swore.

Merle paused for a moment, then continued to kiss him, soft, velvet kisses leading along his ribs to his belly, following the line of hair down. She undid the tie of his robe and pushed it aside, kissing across the flat of his stomach, and he felt the warm brush of her tongue against a bruise on his left hip where he'd lain on something sharp. Her lips carried on kissing across

189

his stomach to his other hip.

In spite of his tiredness, his body responded to her. He heaved a shaky sigh. Her mouth continued its trail across him, soft and gentle, her touch showing how much she cared about him and how much she wanted to make him feel better. She shifted on the bed, and her lips brushed his pubic hair, then her tongue traced up the length of his erection.

He caught his breath, his hand touching her hair. "Merle..." It was one of the few things she hadn't done to him in their time together, and he hadn't wanted to ask—not that it had been a problem, there had always been plenty other things to do in bed. Now, however, he wondered if it was the right time. She lifted her head, pausing for a moment.

Then he realised for the past few minutes he hadn't thought about anything but the touch of her lips. He looked up at the ceiling, smiling wryly, remembering how she'd licked the ice lolly, driving him wild—had it really only been a week ago? Even now, when he was in the pit of despair, she knew how to make him feel better.

He didn't look at her, but he threaded his hands through her hair gently. Understanding, she lowered her lips again. And as her warm mouth surrounded him, he finally closed his eyes, thinking of nothing but the sensations she created within him, desire running through his veins, firing his blood.

Afterward, she curled up against him, warming him through, and he dozed for a while, his exhaustion finally taking over.

He woke about an hour and a half later, his heart thudding, his ears filled with the noises and sounds of the day, but Merle took him in her arms and murmured to him, stroking his hair, kissing him and singing to him softly, and eventually sleep took him again.

It happened twice more in the night, and a third time as the sky was starting to lighten, making his eyes fly open with a start. This time, though, he hadn't been dreaming about the boy and the fire. He'd been standing on the edge of a dock, and Merle had been on the ship heading out to sea. He'd seen her pale form standing by the railing, disappearing into the mist, but although he called out to her, she couldn't hear him, and the darkened sky swallowed her up.

No need to have studied Freud to be able to figure that one out. He shifted on the bed, glad he hadn't woken her. She lay facing him, the blue veins of her eyelids visible in the rising light, breathing nice and regularly, completely relaxed. His muscles were sore and stiff. He wasn't ready to get up. He normally only needed four or five hours' sleep, but after such a heavy day, he could easily lie in until eight or nine o'clock. He still had work though, and had set the alarm for six thirty as usual. An hour to doze with her before they had to go. Nice.

Merle woke at a quarter past six to find him in a deep sleep for the first time that night, sprawled out on three-quarters of the bed in a tangle of duvet. Quietly she slipped out and turned off his alarm, then studied him for a while. He'd been restless all night, but now he seemed to be dreamless, his breathing slow and regular.

She went outside and pulled the door almost closed, then walked into the living room and picked up the phone, dialling Julia's number. "It's Merle," she said when Julia answered. "Sorry to call you so early."

"It's okay, I was up. Everything all right?"

"He's fine, but he had a restless night, nightmares I think. He's sleeping now though, and I was wondering, should I let the alarm wake him? I think he could do with a couple of extra hours, but I know he's supposed to work this morning..."

"If he's sleeping, let him sleep. I'll ring the station and tell them he'll be in a bit later today. He's never off sick. They'll be okay with that."

"Okay, Julia, thanks."

"Oh, Merle?"

"Yes?"

"Happy New Year."

Of course, it was January the first. Merle smiled. "Happy New Year to you too."

"I'll speak to you later." Julia hung up.

Merle made herself a coffee, sat and drank it, looking out at the early sunshine and the fantails hopping about on the deck, and the blue pukekos with their red beaks and huge feet wandering around on the lawn. Then she went back into the bedroom and slid carefully under the covers, curling on her side and watching him sleep, wishing she could stay there forever. She loved him so much. Talking to him the night before about having children had been like a revelation. The thought of staying with him, getting married, having kids, growing old together, would be like winning the lottery and finding a genie in a lamp rolled into one, but she knew it was never going to happen. Surely, Ella and all the other women he'd been with had felt the same way too. But dreams of being with him were like the soap bubbles children blow into the wind—if you tried to catch one, it burst in your hands. It would always be like that, until he met the one lucky woman who finally captured his heart. What would she be like? What qualities would she have that would make him finally feel differently about her than about all the women he'd been with? Or was it more to do with changes in himself? Maybe as he grew older he'd be less anti-commitment and he'd settle, like most people had to, and it would be pure luck whichever woman was around at the time.

He was beginning to stir, and she sighed, seeing it all drawing to a close.

He turned his head and looked at her, his face breaking into a smile, then saw how light it was and twisted back to look at the clock. He sat up hurriedly. "Shit, I'm late! What happened to the alarm?"

"I turned it off." Merle worried he'd be angry she'd interfered with his work. "I spoke to your mum, and she was going to ring the station and say you'd be in late. We thought it best you get as much sleep as you could."

He studied her, his face unreadable, running a hand through his hair. Then he smiled. "Actually that's kind of a relief. It was a rough night."

"I know." She reached over and kissed him. "Happy New Year."

His eyebrows rose. "Oh yes. Happy New Year, sweetheart."

They studied each other for a moment, an ocean of unsaid things between them.

He broke the spell, shifting on the bed, moving his shoulders and arms, groaning a little.

"Are you sore?"

"Stiff." He shot her a wry glance. "And not in a good way." As she laughed, he swung his legs over the bed. "I think I'll go for a quick workout."

"Are you sure? Wouldn't you be better off with a hot bath?"

"Nah, I need to loosen up. It'll hurt, but it'll be worth it."

"Okay. I'll put some toast on." She got up and walked around the bed, but as she passed him, he reached out, grabbed her hand and pulled her toward him.

He put his arms around her and leaned his head against her stomach. "Thanks for last night."

She stroked his hair gently. "You are very welcome, Mr. I'm-so-Polite."

He gave a small laugh. "It was just what I needed."

She touched his shoulders gently, brushing her fingers over the scratches and bruises. "I'm glad I was there. I can imagine it would have been difficult on your own."

"Not at all. I'd have drunk the rest of that bottle of whisky and passed out on the sofa."

She laughed. "Well, I guess I was better for your health. Now go on, run a gazillion miles and then maybe you'll feel better."

He planted a kiss on her fingers and let her walk away. She went into the kitchen, hearing the running machine starting up and then the regular pacing of his feet, beginning at a walk, gradually speeding up to a jog and finally to a flat-out run.

At that moment, the phone rang.

Thinking it was probably Julia, Merle answered it. "Hello?"

"Merle?"

"Bree?"

"Yeah, how're you doing? How is he?"

Merle put some bread in the toaster. "Okay. Better now. Bit of a rough night. He's working out, loosening up."

"Good." Bree hesitated.

"What's up?" Merle put down the coffeepot and frowned.

"I've had a phone call from Mum."

Merle went cold. "Oh?"

"I did something stupid, Merle."

"Oh God, what?"

"She asked for you and...I told her you were with Neon."

Merle couldn't get her brain to think properly. "You said I was staying the night?"

"Yeah. She...she flipped. She screamed at me, saying it was my fault, I'd done it on purpose, finding a man for you here, and now you wouldn't go back and she'd be all on her own..."

"Oh no, Bree..." Merle felt breathless with panic.

Bree was in tears. "I swear, Merle, I didn't mean to tell her, I wasn't thinking, but she wouldn't listen to me. She kept talking about the cancer, saying she could feel it eating her, and she was dying and how we didn't care. I tried to make her calm down but she went crazy..."

"Oh God, I'll have to ring her."

"I wasn't sure whether to tell you or not, but I was so upset, Jake said I should ring..."

"It's okay, it's not your fault. It's her, Bree, it's not you."

"I'm so sorry."

"Don't worry. I'll ring her. I'm leaving tomorrow anyway. I'll reassure her I'm still going."

"Let me know how it goes?"

"Yes. I'll be back shortly. Neon will be off to work soon."

"Was he pleased to see you?" Bree's voice was small.

"Yes. I'm glad I was here." Merle smiled. "I'll see you later."

She hung up and stood there for a minute, cursing. She'd said she didn't blame Bree, but she wished with all her heart her sister hadn't mentioned Neon.

She walked through the house and into the spare room. He was running flat out now, but slowed it to a walk as he saw her.

She indicated his bruised chest. "How are you feeling?"

"Loosening up now." He frowned. "Are you all right?"

"Bree rang and said she'd spoken to Mum. Neon, I need to ring her. Do you mind if I use your phone to call the UK? It's not that expensive now, four bucks an hour or something."

"Of course not."

"Thanks." She smiled and walked out, hearing the machine speed up again. She went back into the living room and picked up the phone. Her heart felt heavy, and for a moment, she debated not calling. If Susan Cameron was in one of her moods, Merle doubted she'd be able to pull her out of it. But her sense of duty and responsibility was too strong.

She started to dial.

Chapter Seventeen

Neon had forced himself to move his stiff and tired muscles, and now settled into a regular rhythm, his body loosening and stretching like worked dough. His brain had been in neutral as he began, concentrating on the different parts of his body, but now he felt relaxed and comfortable, and his mind began to drift.

He thought once again about how he'd felt when he turned around at the station and saw Merle standing there, watching him. She'd been such a comfort in the night when he'd awoken from dreams of fire and being locked in places from which he couldn't escape. Her soothing hands on his hair and soft kisses had dispelled the demons and calmed his racing heart.

In fact, at no point, in all the time they'd spent together, had she upset him, annoyed him or irritated him. Quite the opposite, in fact. He found himself looking for her when she wasn't there, turning to her when she wasn't touching him, and asking her questions when she'd fallen silent, just to hear her speak.

He thought about the conversation they'd had the previous night, when he'd asked her if she wanted children. What had she said? *Maybe.* A cautious answer.

A month ago, he would have laughed out loud if anyone had mentioned him having kids. Even though he knew it would probably happen one day, he couldn't picture himself as a father. No, that wasn't true—sometimes, when he was playing rugby or surfing, he could imagine showing a boy, maybe eleven or twelve years old, how to copy him, but he had no idea what to do with a girl, and as for babies... He was one of those men who would hold a baby like a rugby ball if it were handed to him. He had no clue, no idea.

But now? He thought about the young boy twisted in the seat belt and made himself remember how he'd felt when the lad held his arms toward him, knowing Neon was there to help him. How would it feel if it were *his* son? Reaching out for him?

It was immaterial really, because to have kids, first you needed to have a wife. And getting married, or staying with one woman long enough to think about it, was something he could never have contemplated before.

But now? He thought of Merle, her curvy figure and pale skin, her beautiful long strawberry-blonde hair, her wide blue eyes, her soft mouth, usually curved in a smile. He knew he could picture growing old with her. The thought of being with her day in, day out, was an attraction, not something to recoil from. And suddenly the idea of babies, of her being pregnant with his child, wasn't scary but filled him with a glow he'd never felt before.

He slowed the running machine, walking for a few minutes. He needed to talk to her about this. There were obstacles, sure, but they'd purposefully ignored the subject of the future and trod around it as if it were a land mine, and that was no longer possible. They had to find the mine and disarm it—detonate it, if they had to, anything to get it out of the way and leave the future clear. He wasn't sure what he was feeling. They'd only known each other a few days. But he knew he couldn't let her go.

He bounced off the end of the machine and stopped it, grabbed a towel and, excitement rising in him, left the room.

The conversation was not going well.

Merle sighed and stood. She walked over to the large windows, looking out at the garden. The leaves on the trees and the luscious tropical plants bowed under the weight of the rain, mirroring the responsibility pressing on her.

"Mum," she said patiently, "please calm down. It won't be long and I'll be back with you, and then everything will be fine."

"Stop patronising me," Susan snapped. "I'm not a five-year-old."

Then stop acting like one. The thought ran through Merle's head, but she didn't say it. Instead, she said, "I'm sorry—I didn't mean to be condescending. I was just trying to say you shouldn't worry about what Bree said."

"You don't understand." Susan's voice faded to a whisper. "I know I'm a burden on you, sweetheart. I don't mean to be."

"You're not a burden, Mum." Well, what else could she say?

"But I don't have anyone else. And I'm...so scared..."

Merle frowned. "What's going on? What's this all about? Are you feeling okay?" There was a moment of silence, which frightened Merle more than anything. Susan was never quiet, and always took the opportunity of a lull in the conversation to launch into a fresh tirade. "Mum? Tell me."

"I...I wasn't going to say anything until you got back..." Susan's voice broke.

"Oh no, what's happened?"

"I've been having terrible headaches... I called the doctor eventually and...he's sending me back to the hospital. He thinks...he thinks the cancer might have spread to my brain."

199

Susan burst into tears.

"Oh God..." Merle pressed shaking fingers to her lips. "Oh Mum, I'm so sorry."

"No, you're not," Susan sobbed.

"Mum!" Merle gasped, appalled.

"Don't try and pretend like you care." Susan's sharp, cracked voice cleaved through Merle's heart. "Cavorting about on the opposite side of the world with your fireman, with not a thought for me."

"Stop it." Merle was shaking all over now. "That's incredibly unfair. I came here to get away for a while. I work hard, Mum, I needed a break, but I will be back, I promise."

"I don't believe you. You're going to stay in New Zealand and marry this guy and then I'll be here all by myself..." Susan's voice was so high now only dogs could hear it.

"Marry him! Don't be ridiculous. I'm on holiday—and I'm not a nun, for Christ's sake, even *I* like to have sex at least once a year." Merle felt panicky, knowing her mother could work herself up into a frenzy, which could be fatal if, indeed, she did have something else wrong with her. She had to calm her down. "Why would I want to live in New Zealand? England is my home."

Standing in the doorway as he waited for her to come off the phone, Neon had soon become aware this was not a conversation he wanted to overhear. He desperately wanted to turn and walk away, but his feet appeared to be stuck to the floor, and he could only listen as, inside, he turned gradually to stone.

Merle heaved a sigh. "Bree doesn't have a clue how I feel. It's just a fling, Mum. Something to pass the time. He doesn't mean anything to me."

He must have moved, or gasped maybe, because Merle glanced over her shoulder. She froze as she saw him standing there. For a long second—the longest in history—they stared at each other. Then he turned and walked back along the hall.

He walked into the bedroom. His hands were shaking. He picked up the bottle of water on the bedside table and went over to the window. His heart pounded as if he were running flat out. He stood rigid, one hand on his hip, the other holding the water so tightly the plastic bottle crackled in his hand.

There was a sound in the doorway, and he turned toward her. He kept his face carefully blank.

She walked in, stopped, walked forward a bit more then stopped at the foot of the bed.

He waited for her to burst forth, to start talking nervously, to try to explain what she'd said, but she didn't. She faced him, biting her bottom lip, her eyes taking on that carefully guarded look he'd seen several times, usually when she was considering what to say.

He took a sip from the bottle of water, more from something to do than a need for refreshment. He studied her. She was still wearing his All Blacks T-shirt, her long hair tangled from sleep, utterly gorgeous.

"My mum's in a bad way," she said.

He said nothing, the water he'd drunk making him feel sick.

"She was very upset. She needed reassurance."

His heart thumped so hard, for a moment he thought he was having a heart attack. He kept his eyes fixed on her, although he forced his body to remain in a casual, relaxed pose.

Merle took another step forward. She looked incredibly

calm. How could she be so calm? "I didn't mean it," she said carefully. "I said it to placate her. You know I didn't mean it."

"Hey, I told you the first time we met, you don't have to justify yourself to me." He put down the bottle, standing with both hands on hips. "Anyway, it doesn't matter one way or the other, does it? You're going back. I live here. What's to talk about?"

For the first time he saw a flicker of emotion in her eyes. "I didn't mean it," she said for the third time, her voice husky. "You have to believe that."

He shrugged, his gaze on hers. "Whatever."

She swallowed and came closer until she was standing a foot away. Her eyes were dark with unsaid words, and he knew what she was going to say—and couldn't bear her to say it.

"Neon, you know I lo—"

"Don't say it!"

She stopped, shocked. "What? Why?" She frowned. "What's so bad about saying it? Why are you so bloody anti-commitment? Why do you push every woman away?"

His stomach was churning. A minute ago, she'd told her mother he meant nothing to her. Now she was trying to say she loved him? Clearly, the words held no meaning for her, and that was his fault.

"I made a bet with Jake."

She looked puzzled. "What?"

"I bet him I could make you fall in love with me before the end of your holiday." He flicked out his hands. *Ta-da.* "Guess I win."

Her eyes flickered with anger, hurt. "You made a bet? What the hell? So that's all this has been? It's all a fake?"

He glared at her. "Are you going to lecture me on taking

bets? How much money have you made this week?"

She couldn't have been more shocked if he'd slapped her. Her eyes looked deep into his, her mouth an *O* of surprise. Then she dropped her gaze to the floor, ashamed.

It wasn't enough. He wanted to hurt her, to make her feel as bad as he was feeling. "Getting paid for having sex, Merle?" he said softly. "Really? There's a name for women who do that."

He waited for her to yell at him, to scream, to throw something, to do anything that would give him an excuse to feel justified for making such a horrific accusation.

But she didn't. Twin spots of scarlet appeared on her cheeks, although the rest of her face was white. She gave a small, sharp laugh. "Right." Her gaze remained on the floor.

Without looking up again, she turned. Collecting her skirt and bag, she walked out of the room.

He heard her going along the hall and the front door opening and closing. There was a moment's pause, presumably while she pulled on her skirt, then he heard her footsteps on the gravel, running up the drive.

It was the worst day he'd ever spent at work, the worst mood he'd ever been in, and they put up with him until about three thirty before finally sending him home.

He drove to his house too fast, went inside and walked around banging doors, then tried to have a workout, only succeeding in nearly pulling a muscle in his shoulder when he attempted to lift weights without properly warming up. Cursing, he went into the living room, took out the whisky and poured himself a large glass. Drinking it in one go, grimacing, he poured himself another, then sat in the chair by the window and glowered.

Several hours went by, and he gradually got drunk, so miserable he couldn't motivate himself to eat or read or do anything but sit there, cursing Merle, and Bree for introducing him to her, and everyone else he could think of for having a part in this stupid situation.

At six thirty, there was a knock at the door.

"Go away!" he yelled. He knocked back the last half-inch in the glass and poured another.

Whoever it was banged on the glass. "Open up, Neon, I know you're in there!" It was Jake.

Neon walked over unsteadily and yanked the door open. "What?" he barked.

Jake glared at him. "You fucking idiot." He pushed past him into the living room.

"Please, come in." Neon gestured to the space in front of him then closed the door. He walked past Jake to his chair, sat and took a mouthful of the amber liquid. He'd long since given up getting ice.

Jake stood in front of him, fixing him with a heated stare.

Neon shot him a dark look. "I presume you're going to tell me why you swore at me."

"You told her about the bet. What the hell did you do that for?"

Neon looked out of the window. "She was about to tell me she loved me, if you must know, not that it's any of your business."

"And you stopped her with that little revelation? What the hell is wrong with you?"

Neon slammed the glass on the table and stood up. "I overheard her talking to her mother—Merle told her I didn't mean anything to her."

"She didn't mean it, Neon. She's crazy about you."

"If she is, it's because of that stupid bet, because I made her say it. What does it mean if someone else makes you say it?"

"You didn't make her say it, you idiot. You can't force someone to say something like that. So you turned on the charm, romanced her a little, what's wrong with that? It's what we do with women. Can you honestly tell me every single second you were thinking about the bet? Planning what to do next to make it come true?"

Neon said nothing, glowering at his cousin.

"Anyone with eyes can see she's crazy about you, man, and it's nothing to do with what we said that day on the beach. She came here looking for fun, and so did you, but something happened, something neither of you expected. It's nobody's fault, and no one's to blame. It happens. It's supposed to be a good thing."

Neon's heart twisted inside him. "But her mother..."

Jake frowned. "Their mother's ill. She's going into hospital with a suspected brain tumour. That's what she told Merle when she rang. She should have waited until Merle got home—it's only another couple of days, after all, but that's what she's like. She wouldn't have passed up any opportunity to play the guilt card. That's why Merle was trying to convince her she wasn't staying here. She feels responsible for her mother's happiness—Susan lays on the guilt with a trowel. You have no idea what Merle and Bree have been through."

Neon went cold. He remembered Merle saying her mother was sure the cancer was still there, that she could feel it. "Where's Merle now?"

Jake heaved a big sigh. He studied Neon for a second

before saying, "She's gone. She took the five thirty from Kerikeri to Auckland. And Bree's gone with her."

Neon stared at him. "Bree's gone?"

"She's not left me, if that's what you're thinking," said Jake wryly. "Although I am in the doghouse, thanks to you. She's gone with Merle to be with her mother."

Neon sat, his head in his hands. "Oh Jesus." His head was spinning.

Jake swore. "You're drunk."

Neon sighed.

"I'm gonna go. I'll come by tomorrow. Get some sleep. You look like shit."

"Cheers, man."

Jake didn't laugh. He glanced back over his shoulder. "Maybe you'll see sense in the morning." He paused. "I guess Bree's curse came true, eh?"

Neon said nothing. Jake was wrong. Whatever he felt for Merle, it wasn't love. He'd only known her for a week, for Christ's sake. Jake was well out of order.

His cousin walked out the door and slammed it behind him.

Neon sat back in the chair and looked out the window. The pukekos were walking up the lawn, tripping over their big red feet. Merle had exclaimed at their colour, had said they were walking cartoons. It had made him smile at the time. Now he couldn't get his mouth to move.

A while later, when it was completely dark, there was another knock at the door. Neon was dozing and couldn't be bothered to get up. He only realised he hadn't locked the door when it swung open.

"It's me." Julia came in, closing the door behind her. She walked over to him and perched on the arm of his chair. He ran a hand through his hair, looked up at her, then looked away.

"I'm guessing you've spoken to Jake." His voice was croaky and he coughed to clear it.

"Yes, he rang me."

Neon heaved a heavy, ragged sigh. "She's gone, Mum."

"I know, sweetheart."

"Guess I screwed that one up, didn't I?"

She laughed. "Kinda." She studied him, pity in her eyes. "Are you all right, darling? Physically, I mean? That's quite a large dressing on your neck."

"It's okay. Merle cleaned it for me." He cleared his throat again, looked at the glass in his hand. It was empty. He put the glass on the table. He didn't want any more to drink, he'd had enough already.

He looked up at her. "You're going to say 'I told you so', aren't you?"

"No, of course not."

"You should do." He sighed again. "How did you know? That she was different than all the others, I mean."

"It was written all over your face from day one."

"What was?"

"That you love her."

He stared at her, startled. "Love?"

Julia stared back. "Oh no, don't tell me that's the reason you didn't tell her."

"I..." He was having difficulty forming thoughts in his head. "I like being with her. I can't stop thinking about her. I miss her so much it hurts."

"Kind of the definition, sweetheart."

He loved her. He loved Merle. Oh Christ, he was the village idiot. He deserved to be shot.

He leaned forward, put his head in his hands. "I was cruel to her, Mum. I..." He let his voice trail off. He couldn't bring himself to tell her what he'd said.

She leaned forward and touched his hair. "We all say things we don't mean when we're hurting. She'll forgive you."

"I don't know." He shook his head. "It doesn't matter anyway. She's gone."

"So, you're going to give up, is that it?"

He glared at her. "Well, what would you have me do? She's gone back to England."

"Neon, she's not dead. She may be a few miles away, but she's still in the land of the living. Ever heard of a phone?"

"What's the point?" He stood up unsteadily. "She's got a life there, I've got a life here."

"So did Bree and Jake," his mother pointed out quietly. "Sometimes one of you has to give a little more in a relationship. And I know it's doesn't come naturally to you, sweetheart, but in this case it might have to be you." She stood up. "I'm going now. I suggest you get to bed, have a good night's sleep and in the morning have a think about what you want to do." She reached up and kissed him on the cheek. "I'm proud of you, you know that, don't you? You're a good boy."

He pouted. "I'm not fifteen."

"Inside, all men are fifteen," she said wryly. "Now go to bed before you fall over."

Neon locked the door behind her and went to bed as she had suggested. But in spite of all the alcohol, sleep didn't come immediately.

Outside there was a morepork sitting somewhere in the jacaranda tree and he could hear it calling clearly, "More pork, more pork!" Merle had loved the sound, saying it was so much more interesting than all the owls she'd heard in England.

Merle... He thought he'd blown it, ruined his chances. Was it possible there was a way he could win her back? His mother had implied there would be sacrifice involved. He wasn't great at that. He was an only child—he'd led a very selfish life up until now, with no thought of anything but what he wanted and the quickest way to get it, with little regard for anyone else's feelings. Was he capable of being any different?

Maybe it was time to find out.

Chapter Eighteen

The cold January afternoon was dark and depressing. Merle leaned her head against the window of the train and tried to rest, but it wasn't easy. The train was packed, and a couple of families played loud games farther along the carriage, trying to keep their children amused. She had a headache and terrible jet lag, but the noise kept her awake.

Not that she would have been able to sleep much, anyway. Every time she closed her eyes, she saw Neon's face, his eyes cold as he said those terrible, hurtful things. She never wanted to sleep again.

Across the table, Bree read a book, casting the occasional concerned glance across at Merle. Merle had been glad of the way Bree took over the organisation of their travel, directing Merle to the appropriate terminals, finding them taxis, sorting out their seats. Merle had felt like a lost child, permanently close to tears, wanting to go home, curl into a ball in bed and pull the duvet over her head. But instead she'd had to sit on a plane for twenty-six hours, unable to have any privacy unless she went into the tiny toilet cubicle where she'd stared at herself in the mirror, seeing the dark shadows under her eyes and wondering if her lips would ever curve in a smile again.

And now she felt scruffy and in dire need of a shower and fresh clothing. The journey was interminably long, and by the time they pulled in at Exeter St David's, her eyes were scratchy, she had an upset stomach from eating food at all the wrong times, and her irritation level was skyscraper high.

They caught a taxi home, pulled up and heaved their suitcases out the boot. Bree paid the driver while Merle studied the house nervously. They'd let Susan know they were flying home early before they left, but they'd been unable to reach her on the phone at the airport, and Merle had left her English mobile behind when she left for New Zealand. Had Susan been rushed to hospital? Oh God, were they too late?

She walked up the path, past her car, which was still sitting on the drive, and dropped her suitcase, fumbled for her key and fitted it in the lock. Behind her, Bree called for her to wait, picking up her own cases, but Merle ignored her and opened the front door. She entered the lounge, seeing it in darkness, and her heart thumped in fear. "Mum?" She walked through the house, calling, but there was no reply. Clearly, there was nobody at home.

"Merle?" Bree finally appeared behind her in the kitchen.

"She's not here." Panic swept over Merle, making her breathless. "Oh God, Bree, what if she's been taken ill…"

"Let's not get upset until we know what's happened." Bree held Merle by her upper arms. "Come on, you're shivering. Sit down and I'll get you a brandy."

"I don't want a drink." But Merle sat anyway, putting her face in her hands. Her stomach was a tangled knot of emotion—guilt, fear, grief, loss. Bree rattled around in the cupboards, and then Merle felt a glass pushed into her hand. She looked blankly at the amber liquid.

"Drink it," Bree urged gently. "It'll make you feel better."

Merle sipped it and shuddered. It made her think of Neon, drinking whisky on the night of the accident. "I don't want it."

She pushed it away.

"Merle, sweetie." Bree was white with concern and dropped to her knees to put her arms around her sister as tears welled in Merle's eyes. "Oh don't cry, everything will be all right, you'll see."

"I miss him." Merle burst into tears. "I know it's terrible and Mum might be ill and dying somewhere alone in a hospital, but all I can think about is how much I miss him."

"Oh, Merle."

They hugged for a minute or so, Merle's tears soaking into Bree's jumper. They were both wearing thick clothing, and Merle suddenly realised she was warm. The central heating was on. Her mother hated to waste money and always turned off the heating when she knew she was going away, even though Merle told her there was a threat of a burst pipe when she did that. Of course, if she'd been rushed into hospital, she might not have had time to switch it off. Either that, or...

Bree lifted her head. "There's someone at the door."

The two of them stood. A key turned in the lock, and they heard the front door open. They walked through into the lounge, and there was their mother, shopping bags in her hand, a big smile on her face as she saw her daughters. "I didn't think you'd be here until this evening!" She came forward and wrapped her arms around a stunned Bree. "Sweetheart, it's wonderful to see you." Then she came over and did the same to a frozen Merle. "Darling, lovely to have you home."

Merle waited until Susan had pulled back, and then studied her. She wore makeup, and her skin was rosy. She looked healthy and happy. The shopping bags were full of food.

"Where have you been?" Merle said stupidly.

"Sainsbury's." Susan gave her an odd look, pointing to the named carrier bags. "Obviously." She took off her coat and went into the hall to hang it up.

Merle's eyes met Bree's. Bree gave a small shake of her head.

Susan came back in. "I'm going to make Shepherd's Pie for tea—I know you both love that." She stopped as she saw them staring at her, and looked from one of them to the other. "What's the matter?"

"You..." Merle's voice was faint. "You said you were going back into hospital."

Susan waved a hand breezily. "I had a few headaches, quite bad ones. But the doctor said they're nothing to worry about." She looked slightly sheepish. "I'm sorry if I worried you. I was upset when I spoke to you. I...probably got carried away a bit."

"Got carried away?" Merle's voice grew stronger. "You said you were dying!"

Susan frowned. "I was stressed, I got confused."

"Confused?" Merle gave a humourless laugh. She glared at her mother. "You weren't confused. You knew perfectly well what you were doing, didn't you?"

"Merle..." Bree warned, reaching out a hand, but Merle shook her off.

Susan coloured. "I don't know what you mean."

Tears stung Merle's eyes. "I said he didn't mean anything to me because I wanted to make you feel better. And he heard me. He thinks I don't love him."

Susan rolled her eyes and carried a couple of the bags into the kitchen. Over her shoulder, she said, "You've known him what, two weeks? You don't love him, darling, he was just a fling, you said so yourself."

"Mum." Bree's voice was sharp. She looked helplessly at Merle. "God, Merle, I'm so sorry..."

Merle bit her lip hard, but she couldn't hold back the tears that spilled out and down her cheeks. Susan came in for the other bags, glancing at Merle as she passed, slowing and then stopping as she saw the look on Merle's face.

"I loved him, Mum," Merle whispered. "And I threw it all away because of you."

Susan opened her mouth, but nothing came out. She went white, and her lip trembled.

"Don't you dare cry," Merle said harshly. "Don't you dare!"

"Sweetheart." Susan dropped the bags and came over. "I know I'm a burden to you, and you're so wonderful for looking after me..."

"Don't touch me." Merle stepped back. Icy calm settled over her. "I'm done, Mum."

"What?" Both Bree and Susan looked shocked.

"That's it. I'm not going to do it anymore." Merle looked around for her handbag and picked it up, putting the strap over her shoulder. "I'm done being the dutiful daughter."

"What do you mean?" Susan looked appalled. "I need you."

"No, Mum, you really don't." Merle picked up her car keys. "And I've spent way too many years living your life instead of my own. I'm moving out." She walked past them to the doorway.

"You're leaving me?" Susan looked suddenly hunched and pitiful, but Merle hardened her heart.

"You're still my mother, and I'm still your daughter. I can't change that. But I'm not going to be your slave anymore. I have things I want to do—I want to travel, to work abroad, to get married, Mum, and have children."

"Are you going back to him?" Susan asked in a small voice.

Merle swallowed. She still loved him. But the memory of his cruel words and the hardness in his eyes would not be easily shaken. She shook her head. "No, that relationship's done. But there are other fish in the sea." She tried not to think of Neon branding his name into her skin. *Every time you make love to another guy, I want you to think of me.* She shook her head again. "He's not the only man in the world. I *will* find someone else, and I *will* be happy."

She bit her lip. She wasn't going to cry again. "And if you ever want to see me again, or Bree, you're going to have to think long and hard about how you've behaved toward us. You're going to have to change, Mum, if you don't want to lose us both."

She glanced at Bree. "Are you coming?"

Bree smiled. "No, you go. I'll stay and make sure... everything's all right."

Merle nodded. Turning, she walked out of the house.

Nine Days Later

Merle stood to one side of the huge white screen, looking up at an aerial photograph of a deserted medieval village. It was the first day of the university spring term. This was her third lecture of the day, and she was having trouble concentrating.

Focus, she told herself. It was semidark in the lecture theatre, and the students fidgeted, cold and restless. The double doors leading into the room had already banged open and shut several times, and although she liked to teach in a relaxed atmosphere, not wanting to treat the students as if they were still children, even she could get irritated with their constant comings and goings.

As she went to speak, the doors banged again. "Please sit down and stop interrupting my class," she said out loud, without turning around. There was a pause and then the creak of a seat. She cleared her throat. "So here you can see the remains of a village that died out in the years following the Black Death. As you all know, hopefully, if you did my course last year, after the plague swept through England, killing up to half the population, there was much relocation in the countryside as workers moved around, charging more for their services, and as a result many villages dwindled."

Her hands were behind her back, holding the wireless mouse to her laptop, and she now flicked the button with her thumb, changing the picture. "This village in Dorset is a great example, you can see here the grass is lighter in colour, showing stone walls underneath, and here it's darker, indicating some kind of pit." She turned and nodded to the student sitting by the lights, who flicked them back on.

"So, those were a few examples of the ways you can tell from the air that a settlement expanded or contracted." She returned to the podium where she had placed her notes. She checked her watch quickly—she was about halfway through the lecture. Her head ached, but she knew that was probably due to lack of sleep. Perhaps she should have taken the first week off. She shuffled through her notes. It would have been so easy to ask to extend her leave, but it was unsettling for the students not to have their main lecturer there, and besides, she'd wanted to distract herself from recent events.

Now, though, she began to wonder if she'd made the right decision. She sighed, putting the sheet on top that had bullet points of ways aerial photography could help trace the development of settlements. She had to keep going, there was nothing else to be done. "We've talked about deserted medieval villages. Now let's think about towns and how we can trace the ways they change."

She looked up, glancing around the lecture theatre. Most of

the students were engaged, many writing notes, in spite of the fidgeting. A couple were whispering up at the back, but she didn't mind, as long as they were quiet. She glanced over to the right to see who'd come in late.

And then her heart stopped completely.

For a moment she thought she was imagining him. How could he possibly be here, in England, in the university, in her lecture? It didn't make sense. He sat on the end of one of the benches, one arm hooked over the back, watching her. He wore a black, V-necked sweater over a white T-shirt, with dark jeans, and he looked incredibly brown compared to the white teenagers around him. His appearance was completely incongruous in the university setting, like a palm tree suddenly sprouting out of snow. He met her gaze calmly, unsmiling.

She'd been staring so long her students were glancing at one another, puzzled. Several of them followed her gaze, and they nudged each other, pointing to where he sat. He ignored them, his gaze fixed only on her.

She returned to her notes. Her mind had gone completely blank. She stared at her writing but couldn't get her brain to work at all.

She cleared her throat. "Towns." Jesus, what had she been saying? *Deserted medieval villages, aerial photography, yes, that was it.* "We can also trace the growth and decline of towns by looking at aerial photographs of the surrounding landscape..." Her voice trailed off. Her heart pounded, and she felt faint. If she wasn't careful, she'd pass out right in front of the whole class.

She made a decision and gathered her notes together. "I'm sorry, I'm going to have to cut this class short." She didn't dare look up at him. "I'll see you again tomorrow at two. I'll continue this lecture then."

She turned her back on the class and began to put her notes away and pack up her laptop. There was a moment of silence and then the students started shuffling, gathering their books together and making for the exit.

The doors banged shut for the final time, and she hesitated. He was going to be there, she knew. She zipped up her laptop case as his footsteps came down the steps, then turned and saw him leaning against the front bench, six feet away, watching her, arms folded.

"Hi," he said.

She stared at him. Her heart thundered. "What do you want?" She made her voice icy.

He studied her for a moment. "I came to see how you are."

"I'm fine. See? You can go now." She turned and picked up her case.

"Merle... Bree told me about your mother. About how she's been behaving." His voice was noncommittal. Was he sympathetic or angry that her mother had caused Merle to finish their relationship?

She paused, her fingers clutching the case. Her throat tightened so much she couldn't speak.

He continued. "Bree also told me you've moved out. That you've told Susan you're not going to be at her beck and call anymore."

She put the strap of the case over her shoulder. "Yeah, well. She's still my mother."

"I know."

"I can't just abandon her..."

"I know, Merle." His voice was gentle. "But I'm still glad you stood up to her."

She looked at her feet and closed her eyes momentarily.

This was too hard.

"The boy's going to be okay." He cleared his throat. "The boy I rescued. He made it through. I've been to see him. I bought him a Fireman Sam book."

She turned. "I'm glad. Thanks for letting me know." She walked toward the exit.

"Don't go." His voice was gentle. "Stay and talk to me for a bit."

"Talk about what? How my mother ruined our relationship? Or how you insulted me?" Her cheeks burned with indignation. "I don't think so."

"Merle, wait. I've come thirteen thousand miles to see you."

She spun around. "I didn't ask you to."

"I know. But at least hear me out."

"I don't want to. I don't want to listen to you." Anger and hurt threatened to overwhelm her. She felt a mishmash of emotions all knotted up like a bunch of worms wriggling around in her stomach. Anger at her mother, guilt over her relief at finally being free, hurt at the memory of what Neon had said to her, panic at seeing him again. New Zealand had been a stupid mistake—why did he have to come here and remind her of it? She turned to go.

"For God's sake, will you talk to me for a minute?" He stopped as one of the doors opened and a student stuck his head in.

"Miss Cameron, can you tell us what time the seminar is—"

"Get out!" Neon yelled. The student disappeared hurriedly.

Merle stared at Neon, aghast. "What the hell do you think you're doing?"

"I want—"

"It's not all about you, Neon! This is *my* place of work, *my* life. You can't walk in here and do this to me. How dare you interrupt my lecture—how dare you yell at my students!"

He glared at her, hands on hips. She could see him biting back his words. She met his gaze, letting her anger and hurt fill her eyes. Eventually his gaze dropped, and he looked at the floor. "I'm sorry," he said. "I shouldn't have done that."

"No, you shouldn't have." She was close to breaking down. "I've got a job to do—I would never have come into the station and demanded you drop everything and speak to me." She took a deep breath. "I appreciate you flew here and it's a long way and it's expensive, but you should have asked first. My holiday was fun, and I had a great time, but all that belonged to New Zealand—it doesn't belong here. I don't want to see you, and I don't want to talk to you."

He slid his hands into the pockets of his jeans, took a deep breath and let it out slowly. "I'm sorry. Don't go."

She walked past him, pausing at the door. She was trembling, but she knew she had to be hard. "Go away, Neon. I've got another lecture soon, and I need to concentrate."

"Please, Merle. Look, if not now, then later? A little bird told me you sometimes go to The King's Head in the evenings. Meet me there, say, seven o'clock?"

She shook her head. "I can't."

"Just to talk."

"I can't, Neon." She bit her lip, tears pricking her eyes. "Leave me alone, please. I don't want to see you anymore." Unable to look at the despair in his eyes, she turned and walked out the door.

Chapter Nineteen

A handful of Merle's students were waiting outside, but they parted as they saw the look on her face, and she walked through them and along the corridor to her office. Inside, she locked it, sat behind her desk and burst into tears.

After ten minutes, she dried her eyes and put on some face powder and mascara, trying to make herself look decent again. Part of her had thought he would come to her office and not give up so easily, but he hadn't appeared.

She put her head in her hands. On her back, between her shoulder blades, she was sure she could feel where he'd written his name, branding it into her skin. It would be there to the day she died. How could he have done this to her? How on earth could she sort out all the emotions roiling in her brain and stomach?

The past two weeks had passed incredibly slowly. She'd started looking for a place to stay, although as yet she hadn't found anywhere she liked. She didn't have much money saved, and her wage wasn't great. She could barely afford a small flat, and the ones she'd been to see were seedy, damp or right on top of the railway station. Currently, she was staying in a bed and breakfast, but it wasn't a long-term solution.

Bree had flown back after a week. It had been a difficult parting, and they'd both cried. But Bree had told her how proud she was of her for standing up to their mother. Merle hadn't replied. Although she knew she'd done the right thing, it didn't stop her from feeling like a heel.

Bree had asked if she had a message for Neon. Merle couldn't think of anything to say that would make the hurt go away. In the end, she'd thought about the party on Christmas Eve, when they'd had sex in his aunt's bathroom and he'd kissed her goodbye outside. "Just say, 'see you'," she told Bree. "He'll know what it means."

And now she was truly alone. She'd been around to see her mother, just calling in to make sure she was okay, but she made sure she didn't ring every day. It should have made her feel good, independent, free. Nobody needed her anymore. She had no responsibilities and all the freedom in the world. It was her chance to start a new life. And she had no idea what to do with it.

All this mixed with the incredible hurt that swirled inside her from Neon's last words. The pain on his face when she'd told her mother he didn't mean anything to her would always haunt her. And yet it didn't justify what he'd said to her. If he'd let her, she would have explained why she'd said it, but he hadn't given her a chance. To throw the fact that she'd made a bet with Bree back in her face, to imply she'd only slept with him for money, was the ultimate insult.

He'd come all this way to find her, true. But he'd been as self-centred as ever, barging into her place of work, demanding to be heard, yelling at her students. She could only imagine what he would have said if she'd done the same to him. Neon "Feral" Carter. She'd been so careful not to be demanding when she was with him, to step back, to give him no excuse to call her clingy or needy. And here he was, doing the exact opposite to her.

She looked at the clock. It was time for her next lecture. She would have to think about this later. She couldn't afford to ruin her career over him. She still had bills to pay.

Forcing her brain to concentrate on carbon dating and its uses, she gathered up her notes and her laptop and headed out.

All day, she pondered on whether she should meet him in the pub that evening. Her heart pleaded yes, but she knew she shouldn't listen to it. She didn't want to talk to him, didn't want to keep being reminded of how briefly wonderful it had been. What good would it do to go over old ground again, churning up the emotions that had just started to settle like silt in a river? She needed to put him out of her mind. She needed to move on.

So she decided she'd stay in for the evening. Then she got annoyed. Why *should* she stay in? She usually went to the pub after work for a glass of wine and a bite to eat. It made her feel as if she were being sociable, even if she always ate on her own with her head buried in a book. No, she *would* go out, but she'd go to another pub, and he could go hang.

So that evening, at six forty-five, she paid for her glass of Sauvignon and took a seat in front of the log fire, toasting her feet on the hearth. The Green Man was the university local and not her favourite pub, but it was close to her B&B, and the food wasn't bad. It was already half full of students, but they were being fairly quiet, and she huddled in her coat and sipped her wine as she tried to concentrate on her book. Half a mile away, Neon was sitting in The King's Head, waiting for her. She stomped on the guilt that threatened to rise within her. She'd told him she wasn't going. If he was there, waiting, it was his fault for not taking no for an answer. Arrogant ass.

She stared into the flames and tried not to think about how

the warmth of the fire reminded her of the New Zealand sun, its rays hot on her arms as she'd leant on the edge of the swimming pool and studied Neon, his body glistening with droplets, his tattoo curling around his arm like a fern. She shook her head crossly and forced her eyes to focus on the book. Developments in dendrochronology. That was bound to eradicate any lustful memories simmering in her brain.

A noise over at the exit eventually disturbed her thoughts, and she glanced over. A bunch of students were yelling and laughing. She ignored them, returning to her book.

The noise at the door didn't quieten and, if anything, it increased. She glanced over again, frowning. Then she stared.

A tall man, dressed in a firefighter's uniform, complete with hat and a reel of hose over his shoulder, was pushing through the crowd, carrying a portable stereo.

"Did someone order a stripogram?" called the barman.

Merle's eyes widened. She sank slightly in her seat, her gaze darting to the left and right to try and spot an escape route, but it was too late, he'd seen her. How had he found her?

Neon strode over, the crowd parting for him, cheering. He put the stereo on the bar and turned it on. "Come Together" by The Beatles started playing. It was one of the songs he'd played to her on his guitar, following it by telling her he wanted them to do what the title ordered. She blushed to think about it, sinking even farther in her seat, hiding in the collar of her coat, trying to ignore the cheering students.

He turned to face her. His eyes were alight with the mischievous look she remembered so well. He pulled the reel off his shoulder and handed it to her. "Can you hold my hose for me, sweetheart?"

Merle stuffed her hands in her pockets and closed her eyes momentarily. This wasn't happening.

Hanging the hose on her chair, he took off his hat and put it on the table. As the rhythm of the song kicked in, he started to move to the music. The girls in the crowd cheered. Neon shot them an amused look but stood before Merle, moving his hips. She had to look at him—there was nowhere else to look. It was the first time she'd seen him dance, and he had incredible rhythm. She sighed, leaning an elbow on the table, massaging her forehead with a hand.

Very slowly, he pulled off the massive gloves he was wearing and threw them in her lap. Somewhere in the crowd, a girl screamed and everyone laughed.

She glared at him. "What *are* you doing?"

"Bringing you a bit of New Zealand."

She realised he was referring to her comment at the university, *My holiday was fun, and I had a great time, but all that belonged to New Zealand—it doesn't belong here.*

"How did you know I'd be here?" she said, puzzled.

"Followed you."

"You followed me?" she said indignantly.

He rolled his eyes. "Will you shush? I'm trying to be sexy." He started to undo the Velcro flap covering the zip of the jacket, very slowly, sliding his finger down, still moving his hips to the music. She sat back in her seat, looking across at the girls in the crowd, who were shooting him admiring glances. She could imagine them planning to ask him for his number when he was finished.

Now his fingers clasped the zipper, and he began to lower it slowly. She stared, alarmed. He wasn't wearing anything underneath the jacket except a pair of red suspenders.

"Neon...stop."

He shook his head. "Not until you agree to talk to me."

She huffed a sigh. He raised an eyebrow and flicked the zipper down completely. Slowly he began to pull the jacket off his large shoulders, rolling them with the music, fixing her with his gaze. As the chorus ended, he let the jacket slide completely off his arms.

A huge cheer went up in the pub. Merle stared, going completely scarlet. He dropped the jacket over the back of the chair beside her and raised his eyebrows.

Next to her, a woman cheered and leaned over, taking a rolled-up five-pound note and tucking it in the top of his trousers.

"Thank you." He pretended to tip his hat. He turned his other hip toward Merle. "Any offers from this fair lady?"

Merle reached out and stuffed the wrapper of her packet of peanuts into his belt.

The crowd booed. Neon put his hands on his hips and fixed her with a challenging stare. She crossed her arms, glaring at him. Suddenly she was tempted to force him to strip the whole way. Serve him right.

He saw the glint in her eye, and his lips started to curve. Slowly, he began to move to the music again. Winding his hips, he stepped a little closer to her. One of the women in the crowd started to fan herself. He hooked his thumbs in his suspenders, pushing them off his shoulders. He slid his thumbs into his belt. Slowly, he undid the loop at the side of the trousers. Then he undid the Velcro band. She met his gaze, her heart thumping. His brown eyes were hot, defiant. His fingers slid to his fly. Carefully, he began pulling the zipper down. He was going to go the whole way, she realised. And she wasn't sure if he was wearing any underwear.

"Okay, that's enough." She stood up and turned off the music. The crowd yelled. She faced him, breathing quickly.

"Are you going to talk to me?" He put his hands on his hips again.

She hesitated. "Neon..."

"Right, that's it." He bent and, before she realised what he was doing, he heaved her up in a fireman's lift over his shoulder, one arm around the back of her knees, holding her tightly.

She squealed, and everyone in the pub cheered. Upside down, Merle's cheeks flamed again. "Put me down!"

"Nope." He turned around carefully, picked up his jacket, then turned back and headed for the door.

"Napoleon Carter, put me down!" She smacked his backside repeatedly, but she might as well have been hammering at a brick wall. She heard him laugh, and she cursed as he passed through the cheering crowd, through the door and into the street. He walked a short way along the road, ignoring the whistles of people they passed, then stopped around the corner, in a quieter street.

"Put me down!" she shrieked for a third time.

"Are you going to behave?"

"Neon, I swear..."

"Are you going to talk to me, properly? Because I can stand here all night if I have to."

She did swear then, loudly, and got a spank on her butt in response.

"Language, my lady."

She sagged against him. It was hopeless. She knew perfectly well he was capable of holding her there until the sun came up. "All right, I'll talk to you. Just, please, put me down."

He bent and lowered her feet to the ground, pushing her up. She stepped back, straightening her clothes, red and flustered. He pulled on the jacket he was holding in his hand.

"Finished embarrassing yourself?" she said sarcastically.

"Too right—it's fucking freezing out here."

In spite of her fury at him, she had to give a short laugh. "You are certifiable."

"Thank you." He did up the zip and stuffed his hands in his pockets. He studied her, his eyes mischievous. "I would have done it, you know. Gone all the way. For you."

"I know." She sighed. "Why on earth did you do this?"

"Hey, a guy's got to work with his good points. I'm not stupid, I know what mine are."

She studied him, her anger dissipating. "Don't underestimate yourself, Neon. You have other good points, ones not related to physique and occupation."

He raised an eyebrow.

"You're sensitive and thoughtful and brave. Although they may not be the sort of things prized in a Kiwi man, you have them, in large measure."

"No I don't. I'm selfish and arrogant and completely inconsiderate."

"Well, that as well."

He heaved a sigh. She frowned. "Look, as I said at the university, I'm touched you came all this way, but you can't walk into my life and expect me to drop everything for you, it doesn't work like that."

He stepped forward and fixed her with his brown-eyed stare. "Why don't you let me talk? You did promise."

She sighed. "Okay. The floor's yours."

Neon studied her. There was so much to say that suddenly

he couldn't think where to start.

She raised an eyebrow. "Speechless? That's a first."

"It's not easy. I don't do it very often."

"What?"

"Apologise."

She tipped her head, amusement in her eyes.

He took a deep breath. "I'm sorry. Firstly, I'm sorry for turning up at the university, that was stupid, I was going for a cheap shot. I wanted to shock you, but I didn't mean to upset you. I shouldn't have done it. You're right, you would never have done it to me, and whatever I am, I wouldn't call myself a hypocrite."

Her eyes softened. "No, I'll agree with that."

He heaved another sigh. "Secondly, I'm sorry for what I said the last time we were together."

She met his gaze. "You practically called me a whore."

He swallowed. "I know. I wanted to hurt you. Because—and this is the important bit—this is the bit you need to focus on—I was about to talk to you about us. About where we were going."

Her eyes widened. "Seriously?"

"Cross my heart." He did so with a finger, then stuffed his hand back in his pocket. Jeez, this was a cold country. "And then I heard you speaking to your mum and it was...it was a shock, that's all. I mean, come on, like I really meant what I said—I still glow at the thought you chose me that day on the beach. What guy wouldn't be stoked with a compliment like that? I'm so glad Bree pushed you into saying something."

She didn't smile, but her eyes were definitely warmer.

Encouraged, he continued. "While I was running that morning, I was thinking about how much I liked being with you and I realised...I couldn't bear the thought of you not being

229

there."

She bit her bottom lip. He looked at it for a moment, remembering how soft it was to kiss. Then he dragged his gaze back to hers. "That brings me to the third apology. I'm sorry..." He took a deep breath. "For not telling you I love you."

She couldn't have looked more shocked if he'd told her he was gay. "What?"

He brought his hand out to scratch his nose, then returned it to his pocket. "It sounds a bit odd because I've never said it to anyone before. Apart from my mother." He cleared his throat. "Jake said it took him thirty minutes to fall in love with Bree. I'd say it was about thirty seconds for me. The moment I saw you on the beach, I knew I wanted you."

"You fell off your surfboard," she sniffed.

"Well, your skirt was completely see-through, and you have the longest legs I've ever seen."

She looked startled. "Oh my God. That's the last time I'll be wearing that dress."

He sighed. "I love you, Merle. I want to be with you, I want to have kids with you, I want to grow old with you. I don't want to leave you for a second. I'm gonna be such a pain in the ass, you'll be sick of me. See, I can be romantic." He fumbled in his pocket then pulled out the small box he'd bought the day before in Hatton Garden.

He opened the box, exposing the beautiful diamond ring. Dropping onto one knee, he said, "Merle Cameron, will you marry me?"

Merle stared at him. She blinked. "Are you kidding me?"

He blew on his spare hand and put it back in his pocket. "That's not quite the reaction I was hoping for."

"Neon, get up."

He did so, frowning. She was shaking. "Are you cold?" She shook her head, and he realised she was shaking because of what he'd said. He reached out and touched her cheek. "What's up? Don't you want to marry me?"

Tears came into her eyes. "You really mean it?"

His lips curved. "Of course I do."

"Oh God." She shook her head. "I told Mum this was what I wanted, marriage and kids, but deep down, I didn't really think it would happen. I thought I'd lost you. I believed I'd go back to her eventually, and I think she believes it too. I just feel so...guilty." A tear spilled down her cheek.

Slipping the box back into his pocket, he pulled her into his arms. "Oh, sweetheart. I'm so sorry. She should never have put you in that position. It was incredibly unfair of her. You've nothing to feel guilty about."

She rested her forehead on his shoulder, the tears flowing. He kissed her hair. "You're the kindest, most unselfish person I know. But you completely did the right thing. You shouldn't sacrifice your own happiness for her." He pulled back and lifted her face up. "But I don't expect you to move away from your home. I'll move here, Merle. I'll get a job here as a firefighter. I've already spoken to the station back home. They'll write me a terrific reference and John knows someone in Plymouth—I know it's a bit far from Exeter but it's better than nothing. We can live halfway between the two cities."

She went pale, her holiday tan fading with her shock. "You'd move here, for me?"

"I'd do anything for you, Merle." He smiled. "I've never been in love before. It just took me a while to realise it."

She bit her lip. A tear rolled down her cheek.

"Don't cry." He cupped her face and brushed the wetness away with his thumb. His beautiful brown eyes were so warm.

"I can't help it." Another tear joined the first. His hands were icy, the first time she had ever known them cold. Neon and wintry climates didn't go together. He was like a mountain lion that had found itself in Alaska. He adored the heat and the warmth. England was beautiful, its history incomparable, but he'd hate it after a while. He'd miss the space and the sun, the surf and the rugby. She thought of the tattoo on his arm. The country was engraved into his skin. She wouldn't be able to separate him from it. "Neon..."

He bent his head and kissed her. His lips were cold but soft, and his tongue, when it brushed hers, was warm. She sighed, accepting the kiss.

He pulled back, smiling at her.

"Look..."

He kissed her again, longer this time, his hand slipping through her hair to cup the back of her head, pulling her close so he could deepen the kiss. She pressed her hands against his chest, her heart beginning to pound.

"Neon..." she said when she could finally push herself away.

"I'm going to keep kissing you until you say yes." He lowered his lips again.

She slipped her hand between his lips and hers. "Just wait a second."

He frowned, pulling back.

She looked up at him, remembering how sad he'd been that night after the accident, realising a good measure of his sadness had been because of her. "You can't come to England. You'd miss New Zealand too much."

"I'll do it. For you."

"I know. But you'd grow to resent it." He started to protest and she exclaimed, "For goodness' sake, man, let me speak!"

He stared at her, then pretended to zip up his mouth.

She laughed, shaking her head. "Look." She took his hands in hers. "I'm touched at the gesture—and, yes, it was romantic—that you made coming all this way. And I'm stunned at what you've just asked me."

"But the answer's no."

"Carter..."

"Sorry."

She took a deep breath. "We've only known each other a few weeks. I'm pretty sure I want to spend the rest of my life with you, and from what you've said, you seem to feel the same way. But we don't have to rush into anything. I want you to be sure before you do anything as dramatic as settling down, Mr. Feral." She grinned at his raised eyebrow. Then she took a deep breath. "But, if you really want me, I'll come to New Zealand for a while, and we can get to know each other properly, to make sure it's what we both want."

He stared at her.

She waited for him to say something. After a few moments of watching him blink, she added, "You can talk now, by the way."

He swallowed. "I don't expect you to do that for me, Merle."

"I know."

"What about your mum?" He studied her carefully.

"I love her, and I want to know she's all right. But I'm not going to give up my dream for her. I can visit. And she can visit too. As Bree said, she's not an invalid, and she's got plenty of money."

"And your job?"

She sighed. "I've been thinking about becoming a secondary school teacher for a while. I could take the qualification in New Zealand, teach somewhere in the Northland." She smiled. "I adore your country, Neon. I'd love to make it my country too, and I'd love to be nearer to Bree. She'll be so happy."

His eyes were alight with joy. "You really want to do this?"

"I do."

He smiled. Before she could stop him, he pulled the box out of his pocket again. "Merle…"

"You don't have to—"

He raised an eyebrow and she stopped talking. "Now it's your turn to zip it." He opened the box and extracted the ring. "I still want you to have this. I want to give you something to show you how much I love you. And I want other people to know you're my girl." He looked into the distance slightly as if he was remembering something and gave a wry smile.

"What?"

"Nothing. I think I've got tinnitus. Don't worry about it. Look, will you wear it? We can call it something else until I can talk you into walking down the aisle with me."

"A friendship ring?"

"I was thinking more of a shag-partners ring, but your word is good."

Laughing, she let him slip it onto her finger. "Romantic doesn't come easily to you, does it?" Her throat tightened, but she managed to whisper, "Thank you, Napoleon Carter."

"Jeez, I suppose I'll have to say that at the altar."

She wiped away a tear as she admired the ring, turning it this way and that to catch the light of the street lamp. "Where on earth did you get it? It's lovely."

"Local toy shop."

She laughed. He sighed and put his arm around her shoulders as they started walking back to the pub. "There's something else I've got to tell you," he whispered.

She looked at the ring, smiling. "What?"

"I borrowed this uniform from one of the local stations. I don't have to give it back till tomorrow."

She looked up at him. The mischievous look she loved was back in his eyes. She winked at him. "What's next?"

Grinning, he bent his head and kissed her.

About the Author

Serenity lives in the beautiful Northland of New Zealand with her husband and her teenage son, who wants to be a vet. She would much rather immerse herself in reading or writing romance than do the dusting and ironing, which is why it's not a great idea to pop around if you have any allergies. You can check out her website at serenitywoodsromance.com.

It's bad enough losing the wedding rings, let alone your heart...

Something Blue
© *2011 Serenity Woods*
A *Come Rain or Come Shine* story.

Josh Hamnett is best man at his mate's wedding, and he's determined that nothing's going to go wrong on the big day. That's before ex-girlfriend Kate Summerton appears in the church, looking mouthwateringly good in her tight red satin dress. Her maid of honor's dress.

Ceremony, reception, speeches, the first dance...he's got to go through them all by the side of the woman who still haunts his dreams. And to top it off, she's not wearing any underwear.

Their break-up three years ago was explosive, and Kate was sure she'd never forgive how he behaved. But now all the memories are coming back—the good as well as the bad. As their wedding duties keep throwing them into each other's company, Kate can't ignore the resurging chemistry between them—or the nagging thought that maybe, this could be the start of a second chance.

Warning: Contains sexual chemistry hot enough to turn sand to glass—best read while wearing oven gloves and dark shades.

Available now in ebook from Samhain Publishing.

Love may overcome dark family secrets…
but a grieving ghost could fire the final shot.

Ain't No Sunshine
© 2011 Selah March
A *Come Rain or Come Shine* story.

Boone Butler can shut out the memories that made him a war hero, but he's compelled to follow the Sorrowful Angel's mournful wails back to Harlan County, Kentucky. They can only mean one thing: Delia's in trouble. Even if it's been over between them for twelve long years, she can't stop him from seeing her safe.

Delia Concannon isn't sure if the cries she's been hearing in Bogey Holler are echoes of the past, or portents of more heartache in her future. All she can do is keep running her diner and wait for the next in a long string of misfortunes that started when she fell for Boone. Their love began despite their families' longstanding feud—and ended when Boone's brother murdered her father.

Now Boone has come knocking on her door.

One look, and Boone remembers why loving her was worth defying his family. He still has nothing to offer a woman like her, but he can't stand seeing her living in the shadow of rising danger. Delia's not running, though. Even when the Angel's cries grow louder…

Warning: Contains a snarky best friend, her cantankerous grandmother, a hard-headed hero with a soft heart, too many pick-up trucks to count, and one mention of fried okra.

Available now in ebook from Samhain Publishing.

www.samhainpublishing.com

Green for the planet.
Great for your wallet.

SAMHAIN

PUBLISHING

It's all about the story...

Romance

HORROR

www.samhainpublishing.com